White Cop, Lil Black Gurl

It was never about RACE. It was simply about POWER

a novel

by

Antoinette Smith

STTP Books
Riverdale, GA

All Rights Reserved.

No part of this book may be reproduced or transmitted in any form or by any means, electronic or mechanical, including photocopying, recording, or by any information storage or retrieval system, without permission in writing from the publisher, except by a reviewer, who may quote brief pasages in a review.

This is a work of fiction. The names of characters, many locations, and events in this book are fictitious.

Published in the U.S.A. by Straight to the Point Books
Riverdale, Georgia

Copyright © 2011 by Antoinette Smith

ISBN: 1-930231-42-3 / 978-1-930231-42-9

Editor: Windy Goodloe
Cover Design: Marion Designs
Interior Book Layout: The Rod Hollimon Company

Printing in the United States of America

A Letter From the Author

The books that I write will hit close to home,
But someone had to turn the pain on.
Living with a lot of pain built up
Will do nothing but mess your life up.
You might have a wonderful family and think that you've got it made,
But some of us will even take this pain to our graves.
It's okay to be ashamed, but GOD has a plan for us all.
We weren't put on this earth to walk perfect; we were designed to fall.
And, after that fall, all you have to do is get back up,
And make sure that there is nothing but faith in your cup.
There is a GOD because He made me see
That there is more to life than just worrying about me.
I will open doors for a lot of people
Even if my novels never have a sequel.
You can read my books and say
I, too, can write a book someday!

If you can write a sentence, you can write a book.
Every soul has a story to tell.

Antoinette Smith

From the Twisted Mind of a Gemini

Sometimes, I wish that I'd gotten high
To have sex with the white guy.
No one in the YDC ever knew
How much our secret relationship grew.
I was doing what I had to do to get by,
But then I found out that my life was one big lie.
I thought that he would become a better man,
But being non-racist was never in his plan.
He made me do so many things to him that were just plain wrong,
But I didn't bend or break. I remained strong.
Looking into his eyes, which were the same color as mine,
Almost made me think that I was colored blind.
I never knew that I had so much of him in me,
And the truth I should have never seen.
I never wanted to be a part of his world,
But he was my white cop, and I was his little black girl.

Thanks to publisher Rod Hollimon of the Rod Hollimon Company, cover designer Marion of Marion Designs, and editor Windy Goodloe. Special thanks to El Ranchero Mexican Bar in College Park, GA. Thank you for letting me sell my books, Robert, George, Nacho, and Penguin. Special thanks, also, to Johnny Bailey at Wheels and Tires by Bailey and Big Daddy's Catering and Soul Food.

1
Get Out!

"Get out! Get out!"

Those words played in my head over and over as I packed my bags. Mama had been up drinking all night on Friday while I was in a deep sleep on my twin sized bed. Suddenly, I was awakened by her screaming, "Tasha Jean, get your shit and get out!"

It didn't make any sense for me to say, "Lynn, where the fuck am I going to go at two in the morning?" If I had said one word, she would have beat me, and I would have had to hit her ass right back. I wasn't a bad child, but she had made me exactly the way that I was.

All she ever cared about was sleeping with a different man every other night. I had never met my daddy, and she never talked about him, but, one day, I wanted to find him and ask him why he didn't raise me. She probably don't even know who my daddy was. I am her only child. I used to wish she would have another child, so we could go through all of this hurt and pain together, but I eventually got used to being alone.

I got up and grabbed a few of my clothes and put them in a black garbage bag. As I walked out the door, she said, "My mama put me out at fifteen. You'll be okay."

She had a look of devilment on her face. She didn't smile nor did she frown. She just had a dazed look of confusion on her face. For a minute, she stood at the door, smoking on a cancer stick. Then, I heard the door slam shut. She didn't want to break the cycle. Since her mother had put her out at fifteen, she decided to put me out at fifteen. What sense did that make? I wanted to have a daughter, so I could show her that I knew what love was. I wanted my daughter and me to talk things out instead of fight like Mama and I did. *Where in the hell am I going to go in the middle of the night?* I wanted to go to the Kennedy's house, but, to get to their house on a hill, I would have to go through a dark alley. They were a middle-aged black couple, and they said that I reminded them of their only child who had died in a car wreck. Her name was Sharon, and, every day, I wished that they were my parents. She had been the captain of the cheerleading squad at our high school. She'd had everything! She was spoiled rotten. I had wanted to be her sister so bad. She had all of the latest clothes. She never wore hand-me-down clothes like I did. She even had a car at the age of seventeen.

Then, one day, she lost control of her car on the expressway. The Kennedys dealt with a great deal of pain when they lost her. Everyone at our school was so sad, but her funeral was so nice. She wore a white satin dress with a red sash. She went to heaven in style. I had never ever seen a dead body before, but she looked so peaceful. She looked like she was sleeping. The funeral was so sad. All of our classmates were crying uncontrollably. Her mother had to be taken out of the church. She screamed, "God, why did you take my only baby from me? Why didn't you take me first?"

I went next door to the Johnson's house. Ms. Johnson was a white lady who lived alone with her son Jacob. Everyone called him J.J. He was our school's quarterback. He was very popular, and they were rich. Well, at least, that's what I thought, considering that J.J. drove an Aston Martin to school. His daddy was an extremely successful business man who owned banks all over the world. Ever since he and Ms. Johnson split up, he'd been taking good care of J.J., and Ms. Johnson didn't have to work because he gave her plenty of money every month. Their porch light was off, which usually meant that they were at home. I knocked on the door, and Ms. Johnson answered the door wrapped in a thick red robe. Her initials were embroidered on the front.

"Can I please spend the night? Lynn is having one of her 'get out' fits again," I said as she unlocked the door.

I was crying, and I was cold because it was November, and it was pouring down rain. This wasn't the first time that Mama had put me out. She'd be drinking with one of her men, and it had ended in an argument and that led to her kicking me out. She was always talking about the issues that she had with her mother, who I'd never met, by the way. Growing up, it had always been me, Mama, and her many different men.

"Sure! Come on in. You know where the guest room is," Ms. Johnson said as she opened the door wide.

She was so nice to me, and she felt sorry for me because Mama had made it a habit to put me out almost every weekend, but I didn't want her to feel sorry for me. I just wanted a place to sleep peacefully. She'd always say, "If I could, I would adopt you," but she never did. This shit had been going on for three years, and she hadn't adopted me yet. I knew she just was saying that to show me that she cared for me. Mama should have put me up for adoption when she had me because I would have probably had a better life. I went to the guest room and laid on the queen sized bed. It was so comfortable, and I wished that I didn't have to get up and leave the next day. We lived just south of Atlanta in the country. Some of our streets were dirt roads instead of being paved with concrete.

When I was on my way to the guest room, I peeped in on J.J. He was laying on his back asleep, but I saw his dick standing up through the covers. I went into the guest bedroom to lie down and think of what it would be like if Mama was anything close to my J.J.'s mom.

2
Love Thy Neighbor

When I woke up the next morning, I went into the restroom that was adjacent to J.J.'s bedroom. I was not prepared to see what I saw. He was trying to piss, but he couldn't. He had the hardest, biggest, pinkest dick ever! I stood there for a moment before he looked up and noticed me looking. He then began to pee while looking at me in the mirror. I aimed my eyes on his dick, and I saw that it was still hard. When he finished, he walked by and rubbed his dick against my ass. After I washed my face and brushed my teeth, I joined them at the table to eat breakfast. Ms. Johnson had fixed steak omelets with scrambled eggs, grits, and homemade biscuits.

"I am going over to talk to Lynn," she said as she spread butter on her biscuit. "She has to stop kicking you out."

"That won't do any good," I said as I watched J.J. put salt on his grits.

I'd had a crush on J.J since we were in the fifth grade, and we, at that point, were sophomores. To me, he looked like Robert De Niro in *Raging Bull*. His hair was jet black and curly. He didn't have blonde hair like his mother. He was so cute to me, and he didn't have big, red pimples on his face like most white boys did. His white teeth were perfect, and I loved his smile. It was nice to get a home cooked breakfast because Mama's definition of breakfast was a six pack of beer and a pack of Newport cigarettes. She'd wake me up and make me walk down the rocky road to the corner store.

After we ate breakfast, J.J and I went to the garage. It was decked out like a rock band's studio. The walls were covered with posters of Elvis, Kiss, Rolling Stone, and Bon Jovi.

"I'm going to be a rock star," he said as he threw me a microphone.

He beat on the drums and made the beat to Tina Turner's "Private Dancer". I didn't sing like Tina, but I looked like her, considering how wild my hair was. We sang and had a good time. I didn't want it to end, but it had to because, normally, when Mama had those fits, Ms. Johnson would go talk to Mama and I would go home.

Jacob was the only child, too. He had everything a boy could want.

I looked over at Mama's house, and, usually, when she was awake, the screen door would be open, but it was closed. After we finished singing, we decided to go for a ride on his go-kart on the rocky road. As we went through the house, his mother was pouring herself a glass of wine. She drank, too, but she didn't let it take over her like Mama did. We got in his go kart, and we drove fast. Then, he let me drive. I was having so much fun with him. We rode past the Kennedy's house, and we saw Mrs. Kennedy outside, checking her mailbox. Mama had warned me to stay away from their nephew Spyder. We used to call him Polo in school because all he wore was Ralph Lauren. He had a mouthful of gold teeth, and he had tattoos all over his body including his face. He had dropped out of school and chose to sell drugs.

As we were going back in, Ms. Johnson told us that she was going into town. She also said that she had tried knocking on Mama's door but got no answer. She was probably still hung over.

"Come on," J.J. said as he led the way to his room.

I sat on the edge of his bed and watched him go to the closet and get a Ziploc bag of weed.

"This is the good shit that Spyder has," he said as he sat next to me on the bed. "Boy, you can't smoke that shit. Your mama will kill you."

"She's not going to find out. Besides, she's going shopping, and she won't be back for hours."

He rolled three joints and walked out the room and came back with a bottle of vodka.

"You smoke and drink?" I asked as I sat up on the bed. "Aren't you going to close the door?"

"The door can stay open. Besides, my mother won't be back until later. Let's play a game of strip poker," he said as he grabbed a deck of cards off of his dresser.

I had a feeling that I was going to be the first one stripping. The only cards I knew how to play was UNO. I lost the first hand, so I took off of my shirt, leaving nothing on but my hot pink bra. I took a shot of the vodka, and my chest felt like it was on fire.

"This is some nasty shit," I said as I put my hand on my chest.

He lost the next hand, so it was time for him to take something off.

"Lose those shorts," I said as I reached for his joint.

He took off of his shorts, and, through his boxer shorts, I saw that his dick was hard. I looked down at it, and he took his shot to the head without even frowning like I had. It was time for me to strip again.

"Take off that bra," he said as he grabbed his dick.

I took off my A cup bra, and both of my breasts stood straight up. My nipples were almond colored, and they were the perfect size. He walked over and kissed me. I wasn't shocked because I knew something was about to go down. I looked into his hazel eyes and said, "Have you ever had sex before?"

"Everyone has," he said.

Then, he tongue kissed me.

I had heard Mama having sex plenty of times, and she made it sound painful. She was always screaming like they were hurting her.

"I am a virgin, so everyone has not had sex yet because I haven't."

"Are you serious?" he asked as he backed away from me.

"Yes, I am serious. Have you ever seen me around school with anyone?"

"Well, that just means that I have to be gentle with you."

This is good, I thought because when I did lose my virginity I wanted it to be to him. I couldn't believe it. I was finally going to see what sex felt like. Just as we were about to undress, the door bell rang. I looked out of the window, and I saw a silver BMW. It was Jessica. She was a senior at our school. J.J. insisted that they were only friends, but I knew better.

"What's she's doing here?" she said as he opened door, staring me down. "Did the poor little girl get put out again?"

I didn't like her because she didn't like me. She didn't know me, and she didn't like me because J.J. and I were friends.

"Princeton, bitch," she said as she sat on the sofa.

"J.J., I have to get away from here before I catch a case and whip her skinny, prissy, white ass."

"Just hang out here for five minutes, okay? I will get rid of her."

"Five minutes?"

Twenty minutes went by. I didn't know what they were doing. Maybe, they were finishing our game of strip poker. I went and knocked on Mama's door and still no answer. The sun was setting, so I headed for the rocky road.

3
Wrong Place at the Wrong Time

As I walked, I kicked the dirt and looked at how peaceful the sky looked. The clouds were thick, white, and fluffy, and the sun was just about to set. I got to the end of the rocky road and looked up at the Kennedy's house. Right when I was getting ready to go and knock on their door, I saw Spyder pull up in his gray Lincoln town car.

"You want to go for a ride?" he asked as he rolled the window down.

I looked down at J.J.'s house and mumbled, "Five minutes, my ass."

What choice did I have? Mama wouldn't open the door, and J.J. was preoccupied with Jessica. I opened the door and sat in his smoked up car.

"See. This is why I have tinted windows," he said as he rolled the window back up. "The police can't see when I am smoking on this good shit."

He put the car in park. Spyder had on a Polo hat. He wore it so low that I could barely see his eyes. He had worn Polo in school, and he still wear it now.

"I was on my way to your mama's house," he said as he pulled off. "I don't know why you always run to that racist bitch's house next door to you because she don't like black people. I know the real reason why she's divorced. Her husband left her for a fine-ass black woman. I'm sure you know the rest. Once you go black, you never go back. You need to run with me. I can be your shining armor. You are too pretty to be going through that. I can take you away from all of this. You know what I do, but I have money saved up. I am going to make one last transaction. We can go live anywhere in the world. I am tired of watching my back out here in these streets. I am a smart dope nigga. I move weight. I carry my gun everywhere I go. I'd rather get caught with it than to be caught slipping without it," he said as he got out the car.

He walked to Mama's door and knocked a couple of times. She opened the door, and he handed her a small package, and she gave him some money. She looked out the door and saw me sitting in the car. She flicked her cigarette out the door and went back in the house. He got back in the car and said, "You and your mama have some serious issues, but you don't have to worry. I will take care of you. My mama and I don't talk either."

He cranked up the car.

"That's why I live with my auntie. My mama put me out because I kicked her boyfriend's ass when I found out he was beating on her. It happened about a year ago when I walked in from school. She was in the bathroom, putting peroxide on her wounds. He used to beat her all the time, giving her black eyes, turning her pretty brown complexion purple and blue. I looked at her face and immediately ran to their room where I found him asleep. I pulled him out of the bed and threw him on the floor, and I beat him for my mama's old and new bruises. Then, she ran in there and slapped me across my face, telling me to get off of him. By the time I got off of him, he had two black eyes, a broken nose, and a busted lip. I'd rearranged his face. She put me out the same day, and we haven't spoken since then."

I had no idea that his mama wasn't shit either.

"I have to make a stop at my crib," he said as he turned off the ignition. "Come on in here with me. Let me show you something."

When we walked in his house, there was a portrait of a woman on the wall. It was probably his mama.

"This is my grandma," he said as he pointed at the photo. "I wish she wouldn't have died, but we shall meet again."

He opened a safe on the wall. I instantly memorized the combination. It was not that I was trying to. I was just good at remembering numbers. I could remember my friends' phone numbers from the fifth grade. When he opened the safe, I almost fainted. I had never ever seen that much money in my life.

"How much money is in here?" I asked as I walked over to the safe.

"About thirty million," he said as he grabbed about ten stacks.

"I can't even count to a million," I said as I touched the money like it wasn't real.

"Me neither. That's why I use this money counter machine," he said as he held it up. "It's equipped with a UV light to detect counterfeits."

He closed the safe back, and, as we were leaving, he grabbed an AK 47.

"What are you going to do with that?" I asked as my eyes grew big, staring at the gun.

"Look! If you're going to be my girl, you have to learn to not ask so many damn questions," he said as we walked out the door.

"Well, excuse me," I said as I got in the car.

"We're going to take a quick trip into the city. This is my last and final drug deal. I don't want to go to jail. Hell! The word jail ain't even in my vocabulary. No one uses that word in my car? Plus, I have lawyers on speed dial. I have dirty cops who look out for me. They are known as the old timers. Then, I have those young rookies who are against me, trying to be heroes and shit. They are the ones that are fresh out of the police academy. They're usually the ones looking for some action, looking to get a medal, but I already have two strikes, and I'm not going back to jail. If I go back to jail, I will never see the daylight again or my thirty million!"

He didn't want me to talk, so I just listened to him talk about how much money he had.

"When we get in here with these lasagna eating motherfuckers, you don't speak even if you're being spoken to. We're just here to pick up five kilos of cocaine, and we're going to be out."

"Well, can I just sit in the car since you want me to shut up and just look cute?"

"No, because, if you're going to be my girl, I want you by my side at all times. You can talk. You just need to know to speak on the right shit at the right time."

I couldn't see myself being with him. He was too bossy. I guess the saying is true— If you have money, you pay the cost to be the boss. We pulled up to a gated mansion. The mansion was huge, and, as we got closer, I saw what appeared to be guard men on the outside, holding guns. When we got to the keypad of the entrance, I heard a voice say, "What's the password?"

Spyder said, "Virginia Ann Kennedy"

"You have to say a name?" I said as I looked around at our surroundings.

"That's my boss's way of keeping track of his workers. He knows all of our mothers' maiden names. If we cross him, our mothers will face death. What he doesn't know is that he can kill my mama because I don't care. She put a man before me anyway."

The gate opened up, and it looked like we had just entered a war zone. There were men who wore army fatigue clothing and combat boots. They all carried big guns over their shoulders.

"Now, remember, when we get in here, don't say shit," Spyder said as he grabbed the Gucci duffel bag full of cash.

"Yes, sir," I said sarcastically as I stepped out of the car.

When we got to the door, we were searched before entering. Spyder was searched by a man, and I was searched by a woman. She looked like she didn't speak a bit of English, but she frisked me quickly and mumbled something in a foreign language while she was doing it. When we walked in, one of the men told us to follow him. We walked into a room that was full of men who looked like they were from all over the world, but no one in there was black. We were the only blacks.

"Come on and have a seat," one of the men said. He sat at the end of the table.

He looked like the one in charge. Spyder walked over to him and placed the duffel bag in front of him.

"It's all there, Hector," he said as he sat down. "Do you want to count it?"

"No. I don't have to count out one hundred thousand dollars."

He had a very heavy accent, and he sounded like Tony Montana from the movie *Scarface*.

"I know what it looks like. Besides, you're one of the loyal ones. I've never had to worry about counting money after you."

He snapped his fingers and waved for another man to bring in the five kilos. Hector looked at me. He got up and walked over to where I was standing. Then, he said, "Who is this pretty little angel you have here with you?"

I looked at Spyder. Then, I looked back at Hector. He turned around and said, "Wow! She's loyal just like you are."

"She's my neighbor. I needed some company to come on this long-ass ride with me."

"My name is Tasha Jean," I said as I looked him directly in his eyes. There was just something about my middle name— I loved it! I didn't know what I wanted to be in life, but my name had a little spunk to it.

"She talks," he said as he grabbed my hand and kissed it. "You know you could always come to work for me."

He went back to his seat.

"No, thank you," I said as I looked at Spyder.

Hector looked at Spyder and said, "I thought you were gay because I've never seen you with any pussy around you before, especially not one that has green eyes, curly hair, and a smooth, beige complexion."

Everyone at the table laughed. Spyder looked at his watch and said, "We have a long ride ahead of us. We must be going."

He grabbed the five kilos, and we left.

"After I sell these in the morning, I will officially be out of the game," he said as he threw the five kilos into the back seat.

As soon as we pulled out of Hector's driveway, we saw blue lights flashing.

"Shit," he said as he grabbed his gun. I was about to turn around, but he said, "Don't look back. Why in the hell are they fucking with me? Did you set me up?"

"How the hell did I set you up? I've been with you all day."

He looked at the rearview mirror one last time. Then,

the chase was on.

"What are you doing?" I asked as I held on. "You have to pull over."

"Bitch, if I pull over, both of us will go to jail and never get out. I have enough drugs in here to keep us in prison forever! I am a convicted felon, and, if I get caught again, I will not see daylight again."

He had no intentions of stopping the car, so I began to pray out loud, asking God to please help me make it out of this police chase alive.

"God, please let me make it back home to Mama. If you let me make it out of this, God, I promise I will be at church every Sunday."

"God don't hear people like us. You didn't know that?" he said as he continued to speed from the police.

I was still praying out loud, saying, "God, I'm sorry. Please let me make it out of this ordeal alive."

"Bitch, if you say one more thing to God, I will blow your head off!"

"I am scared as hell," I said as I put my hand on the barrel of the gun.

"Well, bitch, if you're that scared, you better jump out because I'm not stopping!"

We were cornered at a dead end street, and I heard the police say over the bullhorn, "Driver, step out of the car slowly!"

I looked at him and saw sweat bubbles forming on his head. I felt bad that he was going to go to jail forever, but I didn't want to die a virgin. Hell, I wasn't ready to die at all! He looked like he was about to surrender. Then, he turned the car around and put the pedal to the metal. He went full speed at the police cars. The policemen jumped back in their cars, and the chase was on once again. The tires shredded into tiny specks of rubber. Then, Spyder lost control of the car. After that, everything went black.

4
Guilty as Charged

"Tasha? Tasha Jean? Can you hear me?"
I wanted to open my eyes, but they wouldn't open. I wanted to get up, but my body couldn't move. I heard God's deep voice, and He said, "My child, it's time for you to come home."

Fighting to try and stay awake, I suddenly had to close my eyes.
There was nothing but a flat line and a gurney on which my body lies.
Then, I heard God say, "It's not a good idea. No, you shouldn't."
Then, I heard the devil say to God, "I see the cord. Please let me pull it.
I want her to come and burn in HELL with me.
She can join Spyder and be his bride-to-be.
In the flaming fires, that I have so hot,
God, you better not give her life another shot."
I tried to fight, and I tried to hold on,
But God said, "Child, let's go. It's time for us to go on home."
"But I didn't get a chance to tell my mama and J.J. bye."
"Don't worry, my child. They'll all be fine...I DON'T LIE!"
I can't believe that I see myself lying in a casket.
"Why me, God," is all I kept on asking?
"Dying is a part of living, and that's for sure,
But I have unconditional love for you that is so pure."
God, then, told me that he would take care of my loved ones until their final call.
I looked around at HEAVEN and saw the nice place that God has

prepared for us all!!!!!!

"Tasha Jean, can you hear me? Tasha Jean, can you hear me?"

I opened my eyes and saw a doctor looking at me with a face mask on. The light that was shining in my face was so bright.

"Is this heaven? Are you God?" I asked. "Am I dead?"

"No, I'm Dr. Lightfoot, and you are one lucky little lady," he said as he turned off the bright light. "You were in a car accident, and your friend wasn't so lucky."

I was in so much pain. I was chained to the hospital bed. My throat was sore from an oxygen tube. As I tried to say another word, everything went black. Then, out of nowhere, Mama appeared.

"Mama, when did you get here?" I asked as I sat up in the hospital bed.

"I've been here all day, baby. I told you not to get involved with that no good Spyder."

"But, Mama, I knocked on the door, and you didn't answer."

"Tasha Jean, I saw you from upstairs, and I was screaming at the top of my lungs, letting you know that the door was unlocked. I saw you as you got in the car with him, but you didn't hear me."

As Mama came closer and hugged me, I heard the word "clear". I was dreaming. I knew that I had to be dreaming because I couldn't remember the last time Mama had hugged me.

"Hey, there? We almost lost you," the doctor said as he ordered the nurse to quickly add medicine to my IV.

"Do you know your name?" the doctor asked as he

raised my eyelids.

    I looked around the room, and I looked at myself. My brain couldn't register everything at once. I had a bandage around my neck, and my arm was in a sling.

    "You gave us quite a scare," the doctor said as he checked his clipboard. "I wish I could say the same for your friend. There was no saving him. If he'd had on his seatbelt like you, he may have been in the bed next to you, but he was ejected from the car, and he was decapitated. You have a deep cut in your neck from the glass because the car flipped several times. And your right arm is fractured, but it will be back to normal in a couple of weeks. You have quite a few visitors. My nurse or I will be back to check on you shortly."

    Tears came to my eyes when I saw J.J. and Ms. Johnson's faces.

    "Sweetheart, I am going to do everything I can to help you," she said as a tear rolled down her face.

    "Help me?" I asked. "Where is my mama? I want to see my mama!"

    "We have to deal with one thing at a time. You're handcuffed to the bed because you are being charged with drug possession."

    "It's all my fault," J.J said. "If it wasn't for that bitch Jessica, you wouldn't be here right now. You're being charged with possession of cocaine, and they have you charged with two kilos."

    "What? Those drugs belonged to Spyder. I didn't get those drugs."

    "Spyder is dead, and we can't charge a dead man," a detective said as he walked in. Then, turning to J.J. and his mom, he said, "I'll need a moment alone with her."

    "You have to believe me," I said as I looked at Ms. Johnson and cried harder.

"I believe you, and I will get you a good lawyer," she said as she walked away.

J.J walked out with his head down. He looked like he wished he was in the hot seat instead of me.

"Tasha Jean Jones is your full name, correct?" the detective said with an attitude.

"Yes."

"I'm Special Agent Utah, and I will be handling this investigation. I need your date of birth and your address."

"I was born June 3, 1993. And I live on the rocky road by the corner store."

"I know who you are. You're Crazy Lady Lynn's daughter. That lady gets high and kicks you out when she has those 'get out' fits. You're only fifteen years old. Being charged with possession of two kilos could put you away in juvenile for two years. Then, after that, you could go to the big house for eighteen more years. Now, listen, little lady. I need you to tell me where you got the two kilos from."

"Two? It was five," I whispered.

"I'll ask the question again."

When I said five kilos, he began to loosen his neck tie and get a bit irritated.

"Now, where did you get the drugs from?"

"Sir, I was riding with Spyder, and he got them from a man in a mansion that was guarded by heavily armed men."

"Do you know where this mansion is? Do you know this supplier's name?"

"Well, no, not exactly, but I think his name was Henry or Homer or something like that? I know that it begins with the letter h."

"Well, we can't go by what you think his name is or the letter h. Do you know how many people have names that begin with the letter h? We have a solid case, and it's against you," he said as he wrote on his paper.

"Look, mister. I am innocent. I can't go to jail. I have to graduate in two years."

"Well, you should have thought about that before you jumped in the car with Spyder."

"Sir, like I said, I rode with him to this huge mansion, and he paid one hundred thousand for five kilos. I saw him make the trade with my own two eyes. I was right there."

"Right where?"

"I don't exactly know where, but I was in the presence of some crime lords. They all had on suits, and they were smoking fat Cuban cigars."

"Are you calling me a liar? Are you disputing that there were more than two kilos in the car? I was the first officer to the scene of the accident. Hell! I even pulled your ass out."

I knew right then and there that he was the old timer that Spyder was talking about. I remembered what Spyder had said about the old timers who were close to retirement and needed extra money. I bet he was on Spyder's payroll.

"So, what now, Special Agent Utah? What happens to me now?"

"That is left up to the judge," he said as he handed me a sheet of paper to sign. "Your signature means that you stand behind your sworn statement."

He nodded his head at the uniformed officers. And, just like that, I was going to juvenile.

"You have the right to remain silent. Anything you say can and will be…"

My mind went blank. I didn't hear another word as he read my rights. As they rolled me out the hospital, they were stopped my Dr. Lightfoot.

"With all due respect, she has to stay here overnight for observation. She has a three inch gash by her carotid, and, if you don't know what that is, it is the main artery that supplies her blood to her brain. Now, if you'll excuse me, I am taking her back to her room. She has to stay here until the bandage can be removed by me or one of my colleagues. So, have your supervisor to give me a call," he said as he tried to roll me in the opposite direction.

"Doctor, she signed her statement saying that she is responsible for the two kilos that were found in the car," the old timer said with pride.

"I signed what? He told me I was signing my sworn statement."

"Well, my job is to keep people alive, so, like I said, get your supervisor on the phone."

"Oh, my God, what did I do? I can't go to jail for drugs! They weren't even my drugs! Doctor, you have to let me out of here!"

"Young lady, you can't go anywhere with that hole in your neck! I've got an idea. I have a friend that works at the district attorney's office. Maybe, he can shed some light on this situation."

"No, you don't understand. Special Agent Utah is a dirty old timer. There were five kilos in a Gucci duffel bag, and I saw them with my own two eyes."

"Well, I don't know what you saw, but I don't want to hear any more of that. You're disoriented, and the meds are making you say crazy things."

I heard a knock at the door. It was J.J. I was in pain, but, when I saw him, the pain went away. He looked like he'd been crying.

"What's wrong?" I asked as I sat up in the bed.

"Tasha Jean, I have something devastating to tell

you."

"What are you going to tell me? That you and Jessica finished our game of strip poker?"

"I want to apologize to you for that. I feel that I am somehow responsible for this."

"You do?" I said as I grabbed my neck in agony. "You and that damn Jessica. Damn it. J.J., why didn't you tell her to leave? You and I were having such a good time. Now, I'm going to jail for a very long time."

"Tasha Jean, I went to go knock on your mother's door, and she didn't answer, so I decided to kick it down, and, when I went in, I found her. She was dead on the kitchen floor. Her throat had been slashed."

"What? My mama is dead? Are you serious? How? Who? What? When? Why?"

Now, my heart was hurting literally. She wasn't much of a mother, but she didn't deserve to die like that. I cried like a baby, and he came over to hug me.

"Just rest," he said as he patted me on my back. "I am here for you. I am not going anywhere."

I felt good in his arms, and I didn't want that moment to end. A nurse came back in and looked at my neck. She looked at J.J and said, "Sweetie, I will get you a cot to sleep on as soon as I check her vitals."

Then, she walked over to me and asked, "Sweetheart, how are you feeling?"

"I feel like I want to die. Can you just kill me? My mama is dead, and, if I was there, she'd probably still be alive."

"No, sweetheart. If you were there, there would be two dead bodies instead of one. I'm very sorry to hear that, but God placed you in that accident for a reason. God has all of the answers. Just trust Him and continue to pray," she said as she removed the blood pressure cup.

"I didn't want to hear that religious shit right now! Someone killed my mama, and I wanted answers! I want my mama!"

I made room for J.J on the bed, and he held me all night.

5
First Time Offender

After being in the hospital for a month, it was time for me to go face the music. The hole in my neck had healed, and the nurses had treated me so nice. The policemen didn't waste any time. They came and got me once they heard that I had healed.

While I was riding in the back of the police car on the way to the police station, I was thinking, *How much time will I get? At least, it will be for two kilos instead of five, but I don't want to go to jail at all. By the way the detective put things to me, it is as if I don't have a choice. He is so anxious to put me behind bars. If I can prove that he took the other three kilos, maybe I can get him charged with the two that he's charging me with, but how can I win against a sworn dirty officer? Either way it goes, I am going to find out how I can find dirt on him.*

The officers put me in a small holding cell, and I was allowed to make one phone call, but I didn't have anyone to call because Mama was dead.

"You'll get to see your lawyer tomorrow," the officer said as he closed the iron door back.

I looked around the cell. There was a bunk, a shitty toilet, and a dingy sink. *This has got to be hell, and it smells like a Chevron gas station.* I sat on the bunk bed and started to weep for Mama. She was dead just like that. I had wanted to tell her so many times before that. I loved her, but I never told her because we were always at each other's throats. I started to feel guilty, and I wanted my mama back. I was crying so loud, but no one heard my cries, not even God because if He'd heard me or if there was a God, why was Mama dead, and why was I in jail for drugs that weren't even mine?

I couldn't lay on that bunk and go to sleep. I wanted to see Mama and tell her that I loved her. I wanted to see Mama and tell her that I forgave her for putting me out. I wanted to see Mama and hug her and smell the beer on her breath one more time. I wanted to see her smile with that slight gap between her two front tooth. I wanted to just see Mama one last time. I wanted her to scream at me and put me out again. I loved her so much. She wasn't the best mother in the world, but no one is perfect. Now, she was dead with no life in her body, and I just hoped that I got a chance to see her again when I died.

The next morning, an officer opened the door, and in walked Ms. Johnson and a lawyer. She had kept her word and hired a lawyer like she'd said she would.

"How are you holding up, sweetheart?" she said as she hugged me.

"I'm doing bad. I want my mama. Did the police find out who killed her?"

"No, sweetheart. There are still no leads, but the homicide detective said that whoever killed her hated her. He said that, since they took the time to cut her throat, it was personal, almost like she had done something wrong to someone."

"But who?" I said. "All she did was smoke weed, drink beer, and fuck different men. She never hurt anyone but me."

I couldn't begin to figure out which one of Mama's men killed her. There were so many.

"I'm sorry to hear about your mother," the lawyer said as he introduced himself. "I'm Mr. Martin. There's no need to fear Mr. Martin is here."

He sounded like one of those sleazy lawyers off of the TV commercials.

"I've gone over your case, and you have to take the three years. If we take it to trial and you're found guilty, the jury will give you fifty years."

"Fifty years!"

"Yes. Fifty years. Never crank up a jury if you're in the wrong."

"But—"

He cut me off and went on explaining more of my sentence, "Since this is your first time, I can get the judge to give you three years in juvenile."

"Three years," I said as I pounded my hands on the wall. "What if I tell you that a there were actually five kilos and a dirty cop took three of them? Can't you stick him with those two kilos that I am being charged with?"

"Give me his name, and I will pass this information on to my friend who is a private investigator."

"His name is Special Agent Utah."

He opened up his lap top and said, "I'll do a quick search and scan the officers for the Roswell Police Department. Let's see here."

He spelled out the last name UTAH.

"Did he give you a first name because there is no one coming up with that last name?"

"No, he didn't, but he was a detective with a badge and everything. He even told me that he took the other three kilos of cocaine."

"So, you're telling me that a detective by the name of Special Agent Utah confessed to taking the other three kilos of cocaine out of the car?"

"Yes, mister. That is exactly what I'm telling you."

"You could still be disoriented from the accident."

"I am not disoriented; I am in my right mind."

I lied on him because it was my word against his. Plus, he had made me sign a letter that cost me my freedom.

"I saw five kilos in a Gucci duffel bag, and I am sure, as well, when I say that a detective by the name of Special Agent Utah came and interrogated me yesterday."

"Did he give you a copy of the statement that you and he talked about?"

"No, he didn't give me anything," I said.

"Well, like I said, I will pass this information on to my private investigator."

"I think that this is enough for one day," Ms. Johnson said as she stood up.

"But what will happen now?" I asked.

"You will get a court date, and, at that time, you will get sentenced. This charge can usually run anywhere from ten to thirty years," he said as he closed his laptop. "I can easily get you three years in juvenile and maybe probation for about five years since this is your first time getting into any trouble. Now, when you get out, you will have to remain on the straight and narrow. If you get into trouble when you're eighteen, the judge will make you do those five years. When you're a first time offender and on probation, you can't get into any trouble. Do you understand? You're lucky because you are what we consider a first offender. That means that you've never gotten into any trouble. Your charges won't stick once you're released, but, in the meanwhile, try to get some rest and pray that your court date will be soon because the judicial system is so backed up."

"That's easy for you to say. You're walking out into the free world. How can I rest in this place?"

Ms. Johnson hugged me and continued to say that

she was so sorry about everything that I was going through as they left. I looked around the four by six room and started to think back. I wished I could go back to when Spyder first approached me. I would have ignored him. I would have kept on walking down the dirt road, looking up at the sky.

I couldn't sleep in that holding cell. I wanted to be at home with Mama listening to her oldies. I wanted to be anywhere but in there.

Suddenly, I remembered what the man's name was who had given Spyder the drugs. I pulled out Mr. Martin's business card.

"May I make one phone call please?"

"No, you cannot," the guard said.

"I said please."

"Please don't mean shit in here."

I started to cry because she was so mean to me, and I hadn't done anything to her. Besides the fact that she looked like an ancient librarian in the face, she probably needed some dick in her life. Luckily, Mr. Martin returned to my cell.

"I remembered the supplier's first name. It's Hector," I said with the biggest smile ever. "Now that I've given you his name, you can go look for him and charge him with the two kilos."

"Hector Gomez has often been mistaken for a drug dealer because he is a successful realtor."

"Realtor?" I repeated. "Couldn't that be some type of cover up."

He opened up his laptop and pulled up Hector's business. Then, he reached in his back pocket, pulled out his wallet, and showed me a business card with Hector's face on it.

"Oh, my God! That's the guy! He is the one who gave Spyder the five kilos. He even told me that I could come and work for him."

"Sure, he did. You could help him sell houses."

"No, it wasn't about no fucking houses. Quit saying that shit. Spyder gave him one hundred thousand dollars for five kilos. Why me, God? What did I do to deserve this?" I said as I sat on the hard bunk.

"Tasha Jean, take the three years and move on with your life."

He seemed eager for me to do some time, too. I didn't know who to trust.

"Oh, before I forget, sign right here. This is for the three year sentence."

I snatched the paper out of his hand and read it very carefully. I wasn't going to fall for that bullshit twice. I wasn't going to sign a sheet of paper that read I would do ten or twenty years. Sure enough, it was a three year sentence. I signed it quickly and said, "Thanks for nothing."

"I am going to get the judge on the phone to see if we can rush your court date."

"Wait a minute. You have the judge's phone number?"

"Yes, I have it right here on speed dial," he said as he held up his cell phone.

"So, this judicial bullshit is fun and games to you all. Next, you're going to tell me that you and the judge went to school together."

"As a matter of fact, we did," he said as he left.

6
Youth Detention Center (Y.D.C.)

Mr. Martin had my court date to come sooner than I expected.

"All rise," the bailiff said as the judge entered the courtroom.

I was standing there in an orange jumpsuit with shackles on my feet. I looked around and was relieved when I saw J.J. and Ms. Johnson there. Mr. Martin walked up to the judge, and she read my sentence loud and proud.

"Tasha Jean Jones, you will hereby serve three years in a juvenile detention center, and you will also serve five years probation."

After that mean-ass judge banged her gavel, I was so mad at her. She didn't ask me any questions, nor did she look up at me out of those glasses that she had on. I asked Mr. Martin if I could have a word with J.J. and Ms. Johnson. I walked over to them slowly because it was difficult to walk with shackles around my ankles. We all sat down in a room alone. Ms. Johnson decided to speak first: "Well, this is best for you, considering the circumstances."

"That's easy for you to say. You don't have to go live with a bunch of juvenile delinquents."

"I am here for you," J.J. said as he held my hand. "I love you, Tasha Jean, and we will get through this together. I am going to marry you when you get out."

When he said that, I saw several wrinkles form in Ms. Johnson's forehead.

"You don't have to worry about Jessica anymore

either. It's just going to be me and you."

I felt that he was going to be there for me. I needed a passionate man to be by my side.

"Time!" a guard yelled as he entered the room.

"I will write you every day," J.J. said as we said our goodbyes.

J.J. assured me that he would come and see me and be there for me. When it was time for me to go to the youth detention center, I lined up with several other girls. Some of them were older than me, and some were younger than me. Either way it went, I wasn't befriending any of them. I would be going to juvenile as a girl and come out as a woman because J.J. had told me that he'd always have a spot for me in his heart. J.J. stood there with me until it was time for me to get on the bus. He took my hand and held it over his heart and said, "No matter what, you're always in here."

I hugged him so hard. I didn't want to let him go. I knew that his would be the last face that I would see that I loved because there would be nothing but power-tripping correctional officers after this. I was grateful that he showed me so much love. I think that he felt guilty about letting Jessica in on the day that I got arrested. He told me that he'd find out where I was going to be housed and would come to visit first chance he could.

"You'll need a compass and a tour guide to come where all of this new booty is going," a tall correctional officer said as she slammed the bus door in J.J.'s face.

I watched him until he was as small as an ant.

"What did you mean when you said that he'd need a compass or tour guide to find me?" I asked.

"You are a convicted drug dealer and the state is going to make sure they hide convicts like you until your time has been served. We will have you convicts housed in a secluded area, so none of you can use any contacts to run away or break out."

"What contacts? I don't have any contacts. The only contact I had is dead!"

"Yeah, right," she said as she walked to the front of the bus.

"Alright, fishnets! Listen up! I am the head of this program. My name is Ms. Allgood. You will raise your hand to talk to me, and you will address me as Ms. Allgood at all times. Some of you will break and fold up like a boxer who has taken a blow to the nuts, and some of you will be as strong as gorilla glue. I am not your mother, and I am not your friend, so I do not care about your fucked up childhoods. I repeat. I DO NOT CARE! My job is to make sure that you get those three meals a day and to get immediate help to the ones who are here that are suicidal, but, if some of you kill yourselves, you'd probably be better off," she said. She was so cold hearted.

"Now, listen up and listen well. Here are the rules on this bus," she said as she pointed to the cardboard that was taped to the front of the bus. "We have a long ride ahead of us, so I suggest that you get some sleep because, when we get to our destination, sleep is not an option. Now, sit back and enjoy the ride, and, if you talk, keep it to a minimum and whisper," she said as she sat down.

I knew that I wasn't going to like her, and, just by looking at her, I knew off the top that she was a woman who wanted to be a man. She was about six feet tall and brown skinned with cornrows in her head. I sat down next to a girl who appeared to be the same age as me if not younger. She was a white girl with a long scar on the left side of her face. She looked like she was going in for shoplifting or something. My intention wasn't to talk to her. I didn't want to talk to anyone because, after watching the documentaries on TV about juvenile detention, no one in there could be trusted — not even the guards!

I just wanted to get some sleep; I hadn't slept in a long time. I'd been up for about two weeks. I had bags under my eyes, and my eyes were sunk back into my head. As soon as I laid my head on the window and turned my back towards her, her mouth started running like a fan on a sailboat.

"My name is Crystal. What are you going down for?"

"Murder," I said without hesitation and rolled my eyes at her.

"Cool! Me, too. How did you kill them? I used a knife and cut my step-dad from his groin to his throat. Now that I think about it, I could have given him an autopsy," she said as she looked at both of her hands.

My heart skipped a beat. She didn't weigh but a buck o' five. I didn't know that I would be housed with such dangerous girls. All of them were probably bad, and I had just been in the wrong place at the wrong time. I quickly changed my story and told her that I was going down for drugs.

"What kind of drugs?" she asked. "Was it cocaine? I love cocaine."

"Yes, it was cocaine."

"Oh, I love cocaine. I love how it makes your body numb," she said as she rubbed her nose. "Have you tried it? You should try it?" She was talking so much that, once she'd asked me a question, she'd, then, answer it for me. I interrupted her and said, "You killed your step-daddy. Why would you do something like that?"

"It was easy as making a mud pie. He'd been raping me since I was nine years old."

"How old are you now?"

"I am sixteen. I have a twelve year sentence. I have to do two years here, and, when I turn eighteen, I have to do ten years in the big house."

"So, you will be twenty-eight years old when you get out?"

When I am twenty eight, I will be married to J.J. with kids, I thought.

"You are lucky that you only got twelve years for murder," I said as I looked at the deep cut in her face. "I got a lighter sentence because my mother told them that my stepdaddy had been raping me."

"Your mother knew about that shit?"

"Yes, and I wanted to kill her ass, too, but she wasn't there. One day, I had come home, and Ray was in our trailer watching Jerry Springer. That was his name— Ray, and I'd hated him from day one. My mother knew, but she did nothing. This had went on ever since I was nine years old. I knew she knew because he'd tell my mom that, if her mother lived there, he'd fuck her, too. It went on for seven years. Finally, I just got tired of Ray's shit. When I walked in the door, he was watching Jerry Springer, and he said we should go on there because he was fucking me and my tired-ass mother. Now, that's some real Jerry Springer shit! I was so high off of cocaine that I just looked at him. Then, I said to myself, 'This motherfucker is going to die today.' He said, 'Go in there and get me a beer, and come over here, so we can fuck!' I got him a beer, and I also grabbed a steak knife as well. He laid back on the sofa. I handed him his beer, and I went down to unzip his pants. I didn't even get his dick hard. I stuck him in his navel and gutted him straight up like I was opening the inside of a cow. He bled to death right there on the sofa. I took his beer out of his hand and drank it while I finished watching Jerry Springer. Some people think that

Jerry's fake. I am a living witness," she said as she turned to me with tears in her eyes. "My mother should have been the one that he fucked all those years, not me. She showed up at court and apologized, but how do you get seven years of your life back? I didn't forgive her then, and I don't forgive her now!"

After hearing her story, I felt that I had to be a friend of hers. She laid her head on my shoulder and began to cry. I was definitely feeling her pain. I had tears in my eyes, too. *How could mothers not protect their daughters?,* I thought as I held her tightly. I looked out the window and noticed that we were going down a street that was surrounded by nothing but trees.

"What the fuck? Do you see this shit?" I asked, turning to Crystal.

"We're hidden for real," she said.

Then, we both looked out the window as we approached a building that read WE GET THEM RIGHT GIRLS' YOUTH DETENTION CENTER. I had no idea where we were. When we got off of the bus, we heard the other girls who were already there. They were chanting and beating on the windows of their cells saying things like "new booty" and "fresh meat". Crystal and I stood up and walked side by side after we got off of the bus.

"I will kill one of these bitches," she said as she looked around. "If I killed once, I can kill again."

7
Welcome Home, Girls

"Listen up, ladies! Like I said on the bus, I am Ms. Allgood, and everything will be 'all good' if you do as I say. This place is called We Get Them Right Girls' Youth Detention Center. And it's not named that for nothing. We will get your asses right. There's no doubt about that. I run this place, and there is no one you can run to except me," she said as she looked at us all. "We have many rules here, and you will follow them, or you will go to the hole! No exceptions! Here are the rules and restrictions as follows. Number one. No fighting! Number two. No cursing! Number three. No talking when I'm talking! Number four. No fucking! Number five. No sharing food! Number six. Never criticize anyone who is in charge! Number seven. No gossiping! Number eight. No cheating on tests! Number nine. No talking to the warden! Ever! I am in charge, and she has bigger fish to fry! Number ten. This is Warden Kemp, and she's not to be bothered," she said as she pointed at the warden.

"She's right, ladies. She's in charge, and I am here to oversee and to make sure that you're welcomed correctly."

Welcomed correctly? Was this supposed to have been a warm welcome? If so, then these three years are going to be hell, I thought.

"I will say this before I leave you guys. We will have discussion day. Everyone has to participate. Now, for the most part, we're well hidden, which means our disciplinary skills will work just fine and not be interrupted. I firmly believe in getting you juvenile delinquents in check.

Remember, everything you need to get by is in this little black book," she said as she held up the Bible. "By the time you leave here, you will know this from the front all the way to the back. You girls will respect each other at all times. One more thing, each and every one of you will write in a journal daily. Thank you, ladies, for listening," she said as she left. The warden was a short, white lady with long, black hair.

"Now, where was I?" Ms. Allgood said.

"Oh, yeah! Half of y'all don't have any family, so it looks like it's just going to be you and me. From looking at your files, you all are just a bunch of nobodies, so you can forget about your little boyfriends and everyone else in the free world. I suggest that you pair up with a girl who has similar charges to yours and is compatible with you, or you could create an imaginary friend. I don't give a fuck as long as you follow the rules."

That means that I can't see J.J. until I get out in three years, but I can write him, I thought as I put a smile on my face. As I listened to Ms. Allgood, I looked around and saw that the girls there were mostly dykes. They looked just like boys. Some had cornrows and some had short afros.

"Now, all of you new booties, line up, undress and spread 'em," she said with a smile on her face. She slapped on a pair of latex gloves. As I undressed, I noticed a girl with cornrows. She stood next to Ms. Allgood with our uniforms in her hands.

"This here is my helper Sticky Fingers, and she is my extra set of eyes in this place."

There were three new girls in all, including me. Kenya went up first. She bent over and spread her butt cheeks.

"Do you want me to lift up my breasts, too?" she said with an attitude.

"Oh, we have a smart bitch in here," Ms. Allgood said.

"As a matter of fact, I will lift them up for you."

She took her fingers and pinched both of her nipples like she was milking a cow. It looked painful, and I knew Kenya was in pain because she cried as she was twisting and turning them. Kenya was dark skinned with two thick, bushy ponytails. She looked to be no more than fourteen, but her body appeared to be that of a grown woman.

"Do we have anymore smart asses in this bunch?"

Crystal and I stood side by side. Ms. Allgood walked to me and said, "You look like a smart ass. What are you mixed with? Where did you get those green eyes from? Which one of your folks are white?"

"My mama is black, and she's dead, and I don't know who my daddy is," I replied.

"Well, I don't care, and I don't feel sorry for none of you in here. You all did something bad to come here, so deal with it. Now, step up and turn around and spread 'em."

She put on another pair of latex gloves and rubbed her hand in the crack of my ass. I just stood there, humiliated, because I knew if I said something she would have made an example out of me, too. It was Crystal's turn to go up next.

"Get up here, trailer trash."

Crystal walked up, and she didn't frown or anything when she did her strip search.

"How did you get that scar on your face?" Ms. Allgood asked as she got a closer look at her face.

"This is a war wound," she said, looking Ms. Allgood directly in her eyes.

"War wound, huh? Well, you better leave that tough girl shit in those streets. I am the only one passing out licks in here. Sticky Fingers, give those three their jumpsuits."

Sticky Fingers walked over and threw our jumpsuits at us.

"I see now that no one has respect in here. Everyone meet me in the cafeteria. We will have a brief meeting," Ms. Allgood said as she left.

When we got to the cafeteria, we all sat on the floor, and Sticky Fingers passed everyone a notepad and pencil.

"Listen up! I will not repeat myself," Ms. Allgood said as she took a seat on the aluminum table. "There are one hundred girls here, and I can't watch you all, so, if you do something and you think you're getting away with it, you're wrong. We will exercise at four in the morning. You might eat breakfast at five. It all depends on how I feel. You have school from six to twelve. You will then have lunch from twelve thirty to one o'clock. Free time is from one o'clock to three o'clock. We will have journal and discussion day from three o'clock to six o'clock. You will eat dinner from six o'clock to six thirty. We will have count at seven o'clock, and you all will hit the sack at seven thirty. Now, since most of your showers don't work in the cell, you all will have to pair up and take a shower together."

I glanced at Sticky Fingers, and I saw her staring at me with a smirk on her face. I was the cutest out of the new three that had arrived, but I'd be damned if she was going to fuck me.

"Kenya and Crystal, you two will share a cell. And, Tasha Jean, you will bunk with Sticky Fingers."

This is not going to be good, I thought as I took a deep breath.

"I want to be with Tasha Jean," Crystal blurted out.

"And people in hell want ice water. It is free time," she said as she looked at her watch. "You all have about an hour."

Then, she walked out.

"I'm going to have fun with you," Sticky Fingers said

as she walked by me.

"No, the fuck you're not," I said as I stood up.

Crystal came over to me and grabbed me by the hand. Then, she led me to the other side of the cafeteria.

"I really wish I could share cells with you," she said as we sat on the floor.

"Me, too," I said as I looked back at Sticky Fingers and rolled my eyes.

"Well, let me finish telling you my story," Crystal said as she got up to play in my hair. "My mother never knew how to pick good men. She moved a punk in by the name of Josh. She even told us to call him Daddy, and he was in his teens. She was so high that those drugs would make her say anything, but I do remember a good one she had. John was his name, and he made sure my sister and I had all of our school clothes. Kristina is my sister's name. She's grown and on her own, but, before she moved out, it seemed like our family was complete. We didn't know who our real daddy was, but John filled his boots very quickly. We didn't want for nothing. He was a hard-working man, but our mother was a meth party animal. He never touched us in the wrong way. He didn't even spank us. He spoiled us rotten, and I never understood why my mother didn't realize how happy we were. John had such a big heart. Then, one day, my mother cleaned out his bank account. She took out fifteen thousand dollars, and he couldn't handle her addicted ways anymore. She came home that same day with Ray. He raped me on the same day he moved in. When my mother was sleep, he would come in my room and take off my clothes and have sex with me. I tried calling John a few times, but he'd changed his number. I didn't know how to feel at first, but I was distant from my mother. She knew something was going on, but she didn't say anything. She was too busy getting high. It had went on for years and years until, finally, I'd had enough. I got tired of smelling his beer breath when he was on top of me. I got tired of looking at his yellow, crooked teeth. He really disgusted me. Now, the rest is history. I hope he is in Hell somewhere with his dick on fire! Now, what's your story?" she said as she sat next to me.

"I am in here for three years for some drugs that weren't even mine."

"Well, how can you prove your innocence?"

"I can't," I said as I stood up and looked at what she had done to my hair. "I am not a dyke. I don't like corn rows," I said as I started to take them down. "I just have to do these shitty-ass three years and get out and marry the love of my life."

8
The Hole

Once free time was over, it was time for me to go pair up with Sticky Fingers. She was on the top bunk, so I went for the bottom bunk. She jumped down and said, "Both of these are mine. You have to sleep on the floor."

Here we go with this shit, I thought. *Of all the girls in here, why in the hell did I have to be in here with her?*

"Whatever," I said as I moved her out of my way. I didn't want any trouble on my first day, but I wasn't going to get pushed around either.

"My name is Sticky Fingers, and I run this motherfucker. And I want some of that sweet, mixed-breed pussy, too."

"You're not getting anything from me," I said as I headed for the bottom bunk.

She grabbed me by my hair and slung me into the mirror.

"Fight! Fight!" I heard the girls say as they crowded around our cell.

"Kick her ass, Sticky Fingers!" I heard one of them say.

She was on top of me, punching me in my face. I managed to get on top of her, and, just as I was about to punch her, Ms. Allgood grabbed my hand and said, "You haven't been here five minutes, and you're breaking rules already. You just broke rule number one — No fighting!"

"She started it," I said as I stood up. She took a cheap shot at me and punched me in my face one last time.

"Oh!" everyone said.

"That's enough. You're going to the hole."

"Didn't you see her just take that cheap shot at me?"

"I didn't see anything like that. I saw you on top of her."

She grabbed me by my hair and dragged me down the hall.

"Y'all see this here mixed breed is the first to start some shit. I told you. I will put you in the hole for fighting. No exceptions!" She threw me in the hole and said, "This is what happens when you break the rules!" She slammed the door shut.

"I wasn't fighting alone!" I screamed. I looked around the hole. It didn't look any better than those cells that we were in. There were names of other girls all over the walls. Some even had R.I.P by their names. The smell was unbearable.

"Five days," I said as I made my way to the mirror to look at my face. My left eye was swollen and blue. "I will get that bitch back."

I wiped the blood from my nose. I was light skinned, and my complexion only made the bruises show up more. It was cold in there, too. I only had a thin sheet to cover up with.

"I have to report this place. This isn't how we should live or be treated."

I laid on the bed, and, as soon as I was about to close my eyes, the door opened. It was Ms. Allgood.

"This slop is your nutritious dinner."

"What am I suppose the drink?"

"Drink from the sink."

"The sink doesn't work."

"Well, you better drink out the toilet," she said. "I bet

you'll think twice about fighting next time."

    I put that slop in the corner. I decided that I would just starve to death. There was no way I was eating that shit. I looked under the bed and found a notebook that some of the other girls had written in while they were in the hole. The first page was written by a girl named Jenny.

I have to get out of here.
I can't even think or see clear.
I know what I did in the first place wasn't right,
But I wasn't the one who started the fight.
I finished it because I was just there,
But they jumped on my friend, and they didn't fight fair.
I didn't know that I had killed one of them.
I only hit her upside her head with a rim.
Now, I'm in this hell hole all alone.
I will never ever call this place home.
Ms. Allgood doesn't even have a soul.
She is so mean and always cold.
Mr. Knox is no better.
He never even lets me mail a letter.
To all of the girls who are in here after me,
No one is who they say they are. Just watch and see.

    What does she mean? And who is Mr. Knox? I wished we could use the phone. I wanted to call Ms. Johnson and tell her to report this place. There had to be someone higher than the warden. She didn't care about any of us either. I could tell because she stood there and let Ms. Allgood call us a bunch of nobodies.

    The second page was written by a girl name Brittany.

If that cracker calls me a nigger bitch one more time,

*I am going to go crazy on him and lose my mind.
I was just sitting in my cell,
And he just walked in and started raising hell.
I was doing a few push-ups, my normal routine.
"You want to be a boy?" he screamed.
"Sir, I did the crime, and I just want to do my time."
"But you still have a pussy, now? Am I lying?
You're just a black nigger bitch, and I hate you all.
I am your God, and you will answer to me when I call."
He did it again, y'all. He called me another nigger.
I tried to reach for his gun and pull the trigger,
But that only made things worse.
I envisioned myself riding in a hearse.
He punched me in my throat and said, "Bitch nigger boy, you listen to me.
I am Mr. Knox, and every nigger bitch in here won't be free.
No one cares for you, not even God.
If he did, then why is your life so hard?
Now, we're going to the hole, and make it quick.
I don't want that nigger pussy. You can just suck my dick."*

Whoever Mr. Knox was, I sure as hell didn't want to meet him. He sounded like the devil himself. He sounded racist, too. Is this place even legal? Are these people here supposed to be running such a place? The third page I read was by a girl named Renee. It read:

*I am a loose cannon in this place.
I will kill the next person that steps in my face.
I only have a few more months. Then, I'm out of here,
But Ms. Allgood was stopping that — she made that clear.
I didn't do nothing wrong. I was on my best behavior.
I needed Jesus to show up and be my savior.*

She staged a fight for me to be in,
And she knew I was going to kill. I just had to win.
I was only eighteen at the time.
Now, I will be in prison for the rest of my life, doing time.

This doesn't make any sense. Am I supposed to add to this book of hell? Something had to be done about this place. The more I read, the more I didn't want to read, but it seemed to me that that notebook was filled with interesting stories. I was already on my fourth day, and the same shit had happened. I stacked the slop of trays up in the corner. I looked in the mirror, and I saw that the ring around my eye was going away. I looked thin because I hadn't eaten anything. I was losing weight. I used to weigh one hundred and fifteen pounds. I thought for sure that I weighed right at about one hundred pounds now. My eyes were sunken into the back of my head. My lips were chapped and bleeding. I didn't resemble my mama at all. I stood there looking at myself saying, "I must look like my daddy now."

On my fifth day in the hole, I decided to put the notebook up. I didn't want to read anymore of those girls' twisted tales. Ms. Allgood came to get me and walked me from the hole back to my cell.

"You stink," she said as she opened up the cell door. "You will return to your cell, and you will get along with Sticky Fingers."

She left the door open for a janitor to go in and clean the hole. There was no use in me telling her who had started the fight. It was obvious that she was taking sides with Sticky Fingers. As I walked down the hall, some of the girls clapped for me. I didn't understand why the hell they were clapping. I was the one in the hell hole.

"You wanna know why they were clapping for you?" Sticky Fingers asked as I entered the cell.

"No, I don't wanna know why they were clapping, and I don't care."

"They are clapping because the last girl who went to the hole didn't come out alive. She hung herself with the sheet in there."

I looked at her, and I saw that she had taken her hair down. She looked like a girl. Her pants were still saggy, though.

"You can have the bottom bunk," she said as she jumped onto the top bunk. I couldn't believe that she was really playing with my intelligence. I rolled my eyes at her and laid on the bottom bunk.

"My name is Sticky, and what I say goes. I've been here ever since I was twelve years old. I am seventeen years old now, and I run this bitch. You'll soon know why they call me Sticky Fingers, and, no, I am not a thief."

I was not interested in anything that she had to say. She then said, "I like to stick my fingers in tight, little pussies like yours. Whatever I want, I usually get. I'm here for stabbing my mother's boyfriend Ronnie to death in his sleep. He was raping me repeatedly while she kept herself busy at her job."

The more she talked, I started to feel sorry for her, but she wasn't going to stick her little, funky fingers in my pussy. I got off my bunk and continued to listen to her. She was a cream puff, and she used her boy looks and her sexual preference to make herself feel like she was a big, bad wolf. I watched her as she began to cry. *Damn! Every girl in here has a sad story.*

"I want to apologize for the other day," she said as she wiped the tears from her face. "No one in here has ever stood up to me before."

"Where is your mother now?" I asked.

"She's closer than you think," she said with a wicked look on her face. "Where is your mother?

"My mother is dead. She was murdered. Someone slit her throat from ear to ear."

"Damn!"

I had thought that she was in there for stealing cars or something. So far, she was the second murderer that I'd met.

"So, are you Ms. Allgood's eyes in here?"

"Something like that. I have so much dirt on her, the warden, and Mr. Knox."

"Mr. Knox?" I repeated.

"Yeah. He's a racist correctional officer. He's on vacation now, but you'll meet him when he gets back. That's why I run this motherfucker," she said as she looked out the cell. "I have had every girl in here."

"Don't you want to make a difference," I said, trying to put some sense in her head.

"I don't have anything to look forward to. My mother has told me that the only way I will make it is to bully bitches around, so I am walking in her footsteps."

9
Discussion and Journal Time — Day one

"This is not your mama's house," Ms. Allgood said as we all entered the cafeteria. "I am the H.N.I.C around here, and, for those of you who don't know what that means, it means that I am the head nigger in charge." She looked each and every one of us directly in the eyes. "If you need a drink of water, you have to ask me! If you have to take a piss, you have to ask me! If you have to sneeze, you ask me! You are in my house now, and what I say goes. You can leave all your nasty, little habits out there in the streets. We also have laundry once a week. You'll learn that everything we do around here will be once a week. This is called discussion time, and this means you twisted fucks get to read from the journals that you've been writing in. I am not your mother. Please don't tell me your fucked up problems because I have problems of my own. You all have an identification number on your uniform, which means you're only a number to us. We don't put your names on there because we could care less. Now, line up in a single file line, and, out of the ten groups, one girl will stand in the front and pour her little heart out. And this is the only time that you are allowed to curse."

A tall white girl went up first. She grabbed her notebook, cleared her throat, and began to read.

"My name is Kristina, and I wrote down some stuff that happened to my baby sister and I."

Oh, here we go with another rape story, I thought.

"It all started when my mother moved her boyfriend

Jake in to live with us. I was eleven at the time, and my sister Tiffany was only nine years old. In the beginning, everything was peaches and cream. He would take us to K-mart to get the two-toned Icees almost every day. After a few months, though, the funny remarks started to come out of his mouth. He would say things to us like, 'I never fucked a mother and two daughters before'. I didn't pay any attention to him at first. Then, one day, while our mother was at work, he came into our room. He asked me to scoot over in the bed. Tiffany was asleep on the top bunk. He didn't waste any time climbing on top of me. I screamed so loud when he put his dick in me that I woke Tiffany up. She hung her head down to see what was going on. I gestured for her to keep quiet because I didn't want him to have a round with her. She was terrified. When he was finished, he squirted his cum all over me. Then, he walked out of the room, laughing. I got up, ran to the bathroom, and hopped in the tub. Tiffany ran right behind me. She looked at the slimy, white stuff that was dripping off of me. She had a look on her face like she wished that there was something that she could do. That went on for about a year or two.

One day, we were all eating dinner — Mother, Jake, Tiffany, and me. My mother acted normal at the table. She didn't even punish me for flunking all of my classes, nor did she ask me what was going on with me since I was flunking school. She decided that she'd let her boyfriend Jake discipline me. I told him that I would tell her about what he was doing to me, but that only pissed him off more. He punched me in my face. She heard my cries in the other room as she cleaned the table after supper. She knew that he was sexually abusing me, but she didn't care. She knew that we'd gotten quiet all of a sudden. He came out of the room with his shirt off and sweat pouring down his body. His pants were unbuckled. I was balled up in a corner, crying, rocking back and forth. Tiffany ran and hugged me as I cried. She often cried with me. I didn't want him to ever touch her. She was my baby sister, and I was going to do whatever I could to protect her.

There was another time when Jake raped me. He demanded that I call him daddy. I was terrified, and I wanted Mother to come home and catch him in the act, but she never did. He ripped off my clothes and bent me over and fucked me in my asshole. I was crying, but no one heard my cries, only Tiffany.

'Does that feel good?' he said as he pumped harder.

I continued to cry.

I screamed, 'Mother, please come and save me!'

He said, 'Shut up, bitch! She's nowhere to be found, and, when she gets here, I'm going to make her scream like this, too.'

On a separate occasion, Jake wasn't there, and I told Mother what was going on. I told her that her boyfriend was raping me. I even showed her my panties that were covered with blood and shit stains. He had fucked me in my ass so much that I couldn't even hold my own bowels. She didn't believe me. She told me that I was a little lying tramp. There was another time when Mother left Tiffany home with him, and she sent me off to school. He told me that he would fuck all of us, and I made a promise to myself that, if he ever touched my baby sister, I would kill him dead! I walked in on him, and, sure enough, he was on top of her. I ran next door and broke into our neighbors' house and got his AK-47 off of the wall. His name was Wild Bill, and he was known for hunting bears and wild life. We lived in a trailer park, and those trailers were easy to break into. I tapped him on the shoulder while he was on top of my sister.

'Why the fuck are you disturbing me from catching

my nut?' he said as he turned around.

Tiffany's bangs covered her eyes, but I still saw the heavy tears rolling down her face. I hit him in the mouth with the butt of the gun, knocking out a few of his rotten teeth.

'You gon' be sorry you did that,' he said as he spit out blood. 'Tiffany, get up and run to the playground!"

She didn't move.

'Tiffany, go!' I screamed.

She got up and ran out of the door.

'What do you think you're going to do with that rifle?'

'I'm going to kill your ass,' I said as I cocked the barrel back.

'You ain't going to do shit,' he said as he walked towards me.

I fired the gun, putting a big hole in the wall. He jumped back and landed on the bed. Then he said, 'Look. I'm sorry. Okay? I will leave, and you will never ever see me again.'

'You told me that you would never touch her,' I said as I aimed the gun at his dick.

'I lied. I love to fuck little girls like you and your sister.'

'You have our mother. Isn't she enough?'

'What are you going to do with the gun?' he asked as if I was holding a toy.

'Somebody is going to die today, and it will not be me,' I said as I held the heavy gun.

"Okay! Look! I'm sorry. Okay? Please call the police. Please don't kill me. I'm sick. I need help. I need to be locked up?'

'I'm going to kill you. Then, I'm going to kill that whore of a mother of mine.'

'You don't have the balls,' he said as he sat back and

lit a cigarette.

I walked over to him and stuck the barrel of the gun between his legs.

'Wait a minute. You're going too far now.'

I sensed his fear. I wanted to get a broom and stick it all the way in his ass. I wanted to hear him scream. I wanted to make him cry. I pulled the trigger, and the shot gun blast made him fly up against the wall. Blood was everywhere, but he was still alive. He just laid there, motionless. Then, I made out the words that he was mumbling. He was saying his prayers.

'Too late for that,' I said. 'What about all those times that I prayed for you to stop raping me? Then, you had the nerve to rape my little sister!'

I put another bullet in his chest as I watched his eyes roll uncontrollably up and down. I could see straight through his chest because the bullet had went through him and into the wall. I could look through his chest and see the grass outside of our trailer.

"What have you done?' I heard Mother say.

"Look! He's caught with his pants down. I walked in on him raping Tiffany.'

She slapped me and ran to the phone to dial 911.

'You still don't believe me,' I said as I aimed the gun at her face.

'No! I don't believe you. You're nothing but the devil.'

I wasn't going to kill her until she started saying things like how she wished she had aborted me. She even called me a jealous, little bitch. Can you believe that shit? I closed my eyes, and I shot her head off of her body. The 911 operator was still on the phone. I was covered in blood, and I ran to the playground where Tiffany was.

'He won't hurt us again,' I said as I hugged her, not

wanting to let her go.

Everyone was out of their trailers, watching us. They had heard the gun shots. When the police came, they locked me up. My sister is in a foster home, and she will be able to leave once she turns eighteen. The end, and thanks for listening," she said as she sat down.

Everyone was in tears by the time she finished. I was crying, too. That damn Jake got what he deserved. I would have done the same thing if I had a baby sister, too.

The next person to go up was Kenya.

"Hello, everyone. My name is Kenya, and I, too, want to talk about why I am in here as well. I am in here because I don't like my mama. She treats my other siblings different from me because they all have the same daddy. I was a rape baby. She told me that she didn't want to have anything to do with me because I looked so much like my dad. That wasn't my fault, and I couldn't help that. It was four of us in all, two girls and two boys. I am the oldest. She would leave me at home to baby-sit, while she roamed the streets. My name should have been Cinderella because that's how I felt. My siblings even mistreated me, too.

My mom didn't show me any love. All she did was beat me and curse me. She told me that they were going on a trip to Disneyland. She told me that I couldn't go. She said that she was going to leave me with our neighbors. The night before their so-called vacation, she left me at home with them again. They loved sweets and stuff. I made them three gallons of Kool-aid with antifreeze, and I made them all drink it. When she tried to wake them up the next morning, they didn't move.

'What did you do to them?' she said as she busted in my room.

'You mean your three little angels?' I said as I walked closer to her. 'I just made them drink this stuff right here,' I said as I threw the antifreeze bottle at her.

'You what? Why would you do a thing like that?'

'Take one wild guess,' I said as I followed her to the telephone.

'There's no saving them. It says on this bottle that it is harmful if swallowed. And it looks like that the whole bottle is empty. Yolanda, why didn't you just abort me or give me up for adoption? There are women out there that would love to have a child.'

I was crying, but she wasn't. She was trembling, trying to dial 911.

'You never even told me that you loved me, and I am your first born. You should have loved me more. Instead, you walked around here all high and mighty with their dad, and you acted like I wasn't even a part of this family. Mother, that hurts! It wasn't my fault that you were the victim of a gang initiation.'

I looked into her eyes. They were cold. She didn't care that I was pouring my heart out to her.

'But, Yolanda, I will say one thing to you before I go off to juvenile. I forgive you for not loving me.'

She looked at me and said, 'Bitch, you should have drunk some antifreeze, too.'

She sat down in tears, and I felt sorry for her because I didn't know what love was either, but I don't think I would have killed my siblings."

The next person that went up was Sticky Fingers.

"Child, we have heard your story a million times," Ms. Allgood said.

"I know, but can I please say a poem real quick?" she cleared her throat and said, "Here goes nothing."

We're all in here for the same shit.
We practically killed motherfuckers who wouldn't quit.
Fucking, touching, and making us suck their dicks –
That is the main reason why I love clit.
I feel that I am a boy trapped in a girls' body.
I stood up when I pissed in the potty.
Don't nobody care to hear our stories of pain,
But there is always sunshine after the rain.
We can sit here and talk until our faces turn blue.
Nobody else took those lives. It was nobody but you.
They deserved to die is what we continue to yell.
I believe God sent them straight to Hell.
We were just kids, and none of us deserved this shit.
The criminals wouldn't stop; they wouldn't quit,
But we all got the shitty end of the stick.
People on the outside might think that we're wrong,
But that is what keeps me so strong.
I didn't ask for this bullshit-ass life,
But he kept raping me, so I picked up a knife.
I had to stop my pain that hurt so deep,
And I pray that, whenever I die, God will take my soul to keep.
I don't take back anything that I've done.
Besides, in this place, there is nowhere to run.
My favorite chips are Pringles.
And most of you girls know why they call me Sticky Fingers.

  She stood by Ms. Allgood and gave her a high five. Those two were hell together, but I had to figure out a way to turn Sticky Fingers against her. She was hurt, and I could tell.

  "That's enough for one day," Ms. Allgood said as she looked at her watch. "I don't want to have any nightmares about you twisted bitches tonight. Jennifer, meet me in my office."

We all returned to our cells. I looked to see who Jennifer was as she bounced up and practically ran to Ms. Allgood's office.

10
Back in the Cell

Sticky Fingers must have run the joint for real because, when we got back to our cell, it was filled with the smell of weed. I ignored her and laid on my bunk.

"You know you smell this good shit floating in the air. Ms. Allgood is occupied with Jennifer, and she won't be back for hours. You can hit it if you want. Look. I know you're probably still mad because I beat your ass the other day. Can we please just let bygones be bygones?" she said as she tried to pass me the joint.

"No, thank you," I said as I slapped it out of her hand.

She picked it up and said, "You're lucky I'm too high to kick your ass."

I thought about J.J. The only person I wanted sticking fingers in me was him, not some random boy bitch that I didn't like.

"Hey! Do you want to be a boy-girl, too?" she asked as she jumped off of her bunk.

"Hell, no!"

"Well, suit yourself," she said as she began to undress in front of me.

I glanced at her brown skinned complexion and noticed what appeared to be large whips down her back.

"What are all those marks on your back?"

"These scars are old, and they came from some shit that happened when I first got here. It's no big deal," she said as she slipped on her slippers.

She stood there in her tank top and boxers and

continued to smoke her weed like a chimney. I was the type of person that observed my surroundings. I was the quiet type, and, from listening to Sticky Fingers, she just needed a little bit of love. Hell! We all needed love. I wasn't going to let them pull my card. My plan was simple. I was going to do my three years and get out and marry the love of my life.

"I want a dance from you," she said as she walked over and kissed the Nicki Minaj poster on the wall.

She had posters all over the wall. They were mostly of female rappers in skimpy clothing. I wanted her to just shut the fuck up about us. There was no *us*. She walked over to the stereo and put a CD in. It was the rapper Kilo Ali's "Nasty Dancer".

"You need to stop acting all stuck up and get with the program. Now, I am asking you nicely," she said as she took another drag.

I was ignoring her ass because, if she touched me, I was going to kick her ass in round two. I still wanted some get back. She had fucked my face up pretty bad, and she had to pay for it. I had never been in a fight before in my life, not even in elementary school, so I get sent to juvenile on some bullshit charges and get my ass kicked by a boy bitch.

"Look, new booty, you might as well give in like all the other girls do. You can give that pretty mixed breed pussy up, or you can get it took. The choice is yours, and it's very simple."

I took a deep breath and sarcastically said, "You will not get this pussy. I don't care if you were the last boy-girl on earth."

"We'll see when the lights go off."

"I'll pretend that I didn't hear that threat and write my boyfriend who is in the free world."

"If you're thinking about anyone outside of these

walls, you can forget about him. We're all we have, and you can write until your tiny fingers fall off, but he won't receive your letters. Don't you get it? We're isolated, and our minds belong to the three stupid stooges. Now, are you a virgin? Let me know because I have to get some lubricant, so you can take the dildo quietly. Not all girls can take this big dick," she said as she kissed a big, plastic dildo.

I tuned her out and continued to write J.J a letter anyway.

Dear J.J.,

How are you doing? I hope that this letter reaches you in good health. I can't do nothing but think about what would have happened if I hadn't gotten in the car with Spyder. This place is bad. Please tell your mom to report this place. I don't know exactly where I am, but the name of the facility is called WE GET THEM RIGHT YOUNG GIRLS' DETENTION CENTER. Please get on your laptop as soon as possible and google this place. I've already been in the hole for five days, and I found some damning information about this place. Some girls here have even taken their own lives! Can you believe that? This is not right. Somebody has to do something. They have gay girls in here who are known as "boy-girls". They sag their YDC uniforms, and they wear their hair in cornrows. I got into a fight with one of them, and I got sent to the hole, and she's the one who actually started the fight. She messed my pretty face up pretty bad, but I will get some get back. Well, enough about me, what are your plans when you graduate? I know your mother wants you to go to Harvard. I also know that you don't want to go. I know you want to form your rock band. I say go with your heart. Parents seem to try and live their own dreams through their children. Any word on my mother's death? Did they find a killer? Are they even looking for the killer? J.J., I really hope that you're serious about marrying me once I get out of this place because you're all I have to look forward to when I get out. I don't have any one. I wish I, at least, knew who my daddy was, so I could look for him. They call me mixed breed in here, so maybe my dad's white. What do you think? Please write me back. Please let me know that you haven't forgotten about me. I will end this letter for now, but I will never end the love that I have for you.

Love always,

Tasha Jean Jones

11
Discussion and Journal Time — Day Two

Time has been going by so slow. I've been locked up for one year, twenty five days, three hours, and forty five minutes. All of the exercising and schooling was beginning to get the best out of me. I received my GED. Ms. Allgood was still a bitch, and I had managed to keep my goodies to myself and away from Sticky Fingers. I never received a response from J.J. I often wondered if they had even mailed my letter off. I missed him so much. I can't help but think of all the what if's. What if Jessica hadn't have stopped by? What if I hadn't gotten in the car with Spyder? What if I had died in the car wreck? Does everything truly happen for a reason? If so, then I wonder why this happened to me?

"Listen up, fishnets. It's discussion and journal time again," Ms. Allgood said as she hit the cell bars with her guard stick. "And it really doesn't matter who participates. I have a life of my own. I am having so much fun with my girlfriend Jennifer. Now, I will unlock all of the cells, and, whoever wants to tell another twisted story, meet me in the cafeteria. One more thing, I do have good news for some of y'all who are on your best behavior. In a few months, we will reduce some of your time. Mr. Knox and I will decide who will leave and who will stay."

"You better get up and go in there and get some of that shit off of your chest," Sticky Fingers said. "I heard you crying last night. When you cry, it makes you soft in here. Don't nobody care that you miss your little boyfriend. You might get lucky and be one of the ones who gets to leave early, or I might start a fight with you and make you do all of your time here with me. Your freedom is right here in the palm of my hands. I am Ms. Allgood's right hand man."

She rubbed her chin as if she had a beard. I looked her up and down, rolled my eyes, and headed to the cafeteria.

When I got to the cafeteria, the other girls had already formed a line. Everyone had something to say. I sat on the floor and watched the first girl to go up. She was short and chubby with two long ponytails.

"Hello, everyone! My name is Kirsten. I want to drop some knowledge on you first. Then, I will end this with a poem. First off, I would like to say that I'm going straight to prison when I turn eighteen. I am the youngest person on death row. The jury decided to give me life, but I told them that I wanted to die. I took someone's life, and I can't take it back, nor am I proud of myself. The life that I took was my own mother's, and I wish I could breathe life back into her lungs, but I do know that God forgives me, and He will forgive you, too, but I would like to speak to the ones who are getting out. You have a chance. You have another shot at life. You can make it work for you. I've gotten my GED since I've been here, but there is nothing I can do with it in here. My dream was to become a chef because I love to eat as you can see. Now, I'll have to make license plates for the rest of my life. This is not how I saw my future. I really didn't want to kill my mom, but she tried to put me on a diet, and she didn't want to buy good foods anymore. I was just merely shoving her and pushing her around. I didn't know a little push down a flight of stairs could end a life. I am not going to take up too much of your time because I know that you all have something to get off your chests, too. I just want you girls who are getting out to know that you can be whoever and whatever you want to be. And, to the ones who are in here for truancy and theft, you can make it, too. Don't ever let anyone tell you different. This place can make you or break you. The way they treat us and talk to us isn't right. That's why you have to keep your sanity by reading your bibles and having faith. You have to know and believe in God. There is a God! He does exist. We can't see Him, but He watches over each and every one of us. I just wish I had known him when I committed my crime. Are you guys ready for my poem? It's called "I'm Tired".

I'm tired of playing with you.
I want to get back on track
And never look back.
I took her life,
And, no, it wasn't with a knife,
And just when I wanted things to go my way
The devil came and got in the way.
I'm a big girl now, and I do know right from wrong,
And, on that day, I should have been strong.
God, I need you in my life.
My mother was harmless, just a loving, caring wife.
God, I need you in my heart. God, I need you in my mind.
God, who am I kidding? I need you all the time.
I don't know how I'm going to die — lethal injection or the chair.
But I do know that God will be right there.
As time goes by, I continue to see
That God has chosen to use me.
God gave me a sign last night.
And it was for me to get some of you right.
I will minister to each and every one of you.
Please don't be ashamed. God has assured me that it's the right thing to do
I call this life of mine 'Playing the Cards that I've been Dealt.'

Please don't judge me because, deep in my heart, you haven't felt.
If you could've just walked in my shoes for one day, you'd have seen
How all of the other kids used to tease me.
I've been a big girl all of my life,
But I wasn't prepared for the things that took place in my life
Please listen to me and please learn from me
Because, when you leave these walls, you can be all that you can be.

"Thanks for listening," Kirsten said when she finished.

I was crying hard; so were a lot of the other girls. I looked over at Ms. Allgood. She was getting her hair braided in cornrows by Jennifer. She wasn't crying. She didn't even have a sad look on her face. I wanted to go up and talk about my drug charge, but their stories were much more interesting than mine. The next girl to go up was Sonya.

"Hello, everybody! I just want to say a quick poem. This poem is called 'The Neighbor.'"

Family ain't family, and that's no lie.
Whatever happened to neighbors making our kids cry?
You know, get at us when we told a little white lie.
This neighbor of mine had something else on his agenda,
And he made me stir his tea with Splenda.
One day, I had gotten tired of sucking his dick,
So I hurried to the kitchen and made him some tea quick.
I broke a light bulb and poured it in his tea.
I crushed it up into little small particles, so he couldn't see.
The more he drank, the more that I saw
Him begin to do things, such as grab at his jaw.
I didn't want to kill him. You got to believe me,
But I had to. Otherwise, he wouldn't just let me be.

I told his mom, and she said that he was a little slow,
But he made me suck his dick, so how was I suppose to know.
I don't feel bad for him as you can see.
Now, I'm in here for murder in the second degree.

    The next girl to go up was Jennifer. This would be interesting I wanted to know what her reason was for being in here. She was short with a big booty. Every time she walked, she dragged her feet.
    "Well, as all of you know, I'm Jennifer. I have fifteen more months to go. Kirsten, I will take your advice and stop stealing. I'm going to tell a poem, too, but I want to also give you a brief summary on stealing. Stealing was so easy for me that it became a habit. It all started when I was about eight or nine. You know how you go to the store and pick up a candy bar and start to eat it? Or do some of you recall eating a couple of grapes from the produce section? Well, my friends, all of that is called stealing. I found myself picking up bigger and better things at the mall. I would fold a shirt up so small that it looked like a pair of thongs. I was stealing designer clothes, and I would go to the hood and sell them. I eventually got caught, and here I am in here with you guys. I've never been molested, raped, or none of that shit. I had both parents, and both were very loving, but I was with the wrong crowd, and stealing was easy, and the money was coming quick. I could steal the butter off your toast. I was just that swift. I was spoiled rotten. I wanted to fit in with the bad crowd, and look where it got me. My dream was to become a rapper or a singer. I had everything a girl could want. I had not one but both parents. I stress that because there's nothing like unconditional love. They showed me love no matter what. Even when I told a lie, they believed me, and they knew that I was lying. Every time I got caught stealing, they'd always

come to my rescue and bail me out, but, this last time, the judge didn't give me a slap on the wrist. She made an example out of me, and what can I say? I'm in here, never been to that shitty-ass hole. Besides, I love my mentor Ms. Allgood. I will now get to my poem. It's called 'Don't Look Down on Me.'"

Don't look down on me
I've just about had enough
Don't look down on me
Because my life is not that rough
Don't look down on me
I'm doing the best I can
Don't look down on me
I'd rather be with a woman instead of a man
Don't look down on me
I wish I could feel some of you girls' pain
Don't look down on me
But you did it, and you're the only one to blame
Don't look down on me
If you want to make it in here
Don't look down on me
You have to pair up with another bitch and get in gear
Don't look down on me
Being in here has really made me see
Don't look down on me
That this is not how I want my life to be
Don't look down on me
Some things we do we have to do just to get by
Don't look down on me
Look who I am fucking. I can't lie
Don't look down on me
I'm the type of person that makes shit happen
Don't look down on me

I will make it in the real world by singing or rapping.

"Thank you for listening," she said as she went to finish playing in Ms. Allgood's hair.

"Times up," Ms. Allgood said as she got up. "It's time to eat your nutritious slop."

I didn't eat the food in there. None of it! I only drank the milk and the nasty watered down Kool-aid.

12
Frienemies @ Chow Time

We lined up and washed our hands before we went to eat that slop that they called dinner. I got my tray and sat down and just looked at that shit. There was no way I was digesting that. It looked like a fiber burger, and the potatoes were watery and running off the tray. Only the roll looked like it was fresh and hot. I hadn't eaten much. Maybe, a few crackers here and a few raw noodles there. My mouth watered as I watched the steam rise from the top of the roll. I opened up the pack of butter, and, just as I was about to spread butter on my roll, I saw a finger in it.

"What the fuck?" I said as I stood up.

It was Sticky Fingers, standing there with her finger on my roll.

"I saw Ms. Allgood's list, and you're one of the lucky ones," she said. "Now, I been asking you for that pretty pussy for a whole year, and you haven't given it to me yet. So, what is it going to be? Are you going to give in? I promise I'll be gentle."

She licked the tip of my ear. I grabbed her face and slammed her head down on the aluminum table.

"Bitch, didn't I tell you that this virgin pussy is for J.J.?"

She didn't have a chance. I was getting the best of her. Then, I felt a cold hand around my neck.

"Stop it, you black nigger bitch!" It was a man's voice. He threw me on my back and sat on top of me with his hand still around my neck. *This must be Mr. Knox*, I thought to myself. He was pale white with amber green eyes. His teeth were black. He looked so familiar. He looked like the drill sergeant from the movie *Full Metal Jacket*.

"You just earned yourself a trip to the hole," he said as he stood me up by my neck.

"What about her?" I screamed.

"Quit worrying about other black nigger bitches and worry about yourself." Sticky Fingers was smiling as he hauled me off to the hole. I noticed something different as we were walking to the hole.

"The hole is that way," I said as I pointed in the opposite direction.

"We're going to Mr. Knox's special hole," he said as he rushed me down the hall.

I started to have flashbacks of the girls' notes from the previous hole. Some of them had killed themselves because of this man. When we got to his hole, it was much bigger than the other hole. As I looked around on the walls, I noticed that he had posters of the confederate flag. He also had posters of Adolf Hitler and the Ku Klux Klan. He was a racist cracker. There was no doubt about that. He even had a dart board up with a picture of Dr. Martin Luther King's face in the middle. I remembered what Sticky Fingers had told me. She had told me not to cry. I was scared as hell, but I didn't show it. He threw me on the bed and looked at me. He stared at me for about five minutes before he said another word: "Well, aren't you going to cry, nigger bitch? Aren't you scared? Look around. I don't like niggers, especially troublemakers. You're a mixed breed. I can tell by your skin complexion. So, do you got a nigger mammy or a nigger daddy?"

"My mama is black."

"So that means your daddy is white. I would love to

get my hands on him. He must have been desperate to impregnate a nigger bitch," he said as he unzipped his pants. "Get over here. Get on those black nigger knees and suck my pecker."

I didn't want to suck his dick. It was ugly. To make matters worse, he smelled like a wet dog.

"We can do this my way, or we can do it the hard way," he said as he took off his pants. I was about to experience unwanted dick. His dick was long, skinny, and light pink.

"Now, this here dick sucking is non-negotiable," he said as he rubbed his dick, getting it hard. "Open wide."

He shoved his pencil dick in my mouth. I had never gotten the chance to suck J.J.'s dick before.

"If you bite it, I'll make sure you're down here with me for the rest of your sentence. The warden's husband and I play golf together, and I promise you that no one will miss your nigger ass. If you want to see them dyke bitches again, you'll do it right."

"But I've never sucked a dick before," I mumbled with his dick in my mouth.

"Well, you better learn, and you better learn fast. Spit on it. Then, suck it. Then, spit on it some more. Then, suck it some more."

I spit on it, and I sucked it like he said. I couldn't believe that I was getting fucked in my mouth. He held my head tightly.

"Teeth!" he screamed. Then, he slapped me.

"Listen, you little black nigger bitch! If I feel your teeth grind up against my pecker, I will fuck you in your ass with my baton. It's real good for beating niggers! That's why I transferred from the boys' unit to the girls' unit because I got tired of beating those nigger boys. I want you to jack my pecker while you're sucking it. I want to fill your nigger mouth up with my delicious hot sperm. If my wife sucked my pecker, I wouldn't give you nigger bitches such a hard time. About a year ago, I had to take care of some serious business. I had to kill someone, and I am proud to say that that bitch deserved it."

I was jacking his dick faster, but the more he talked, the softer his dick had got. I wasn't interested in hearing him talk about killing anyone. He was killing my throat, and I was ready for him to finish. I felt like I had died and gone to hell. His dick had gotten hard again, and he was jacking it with me. Then, I saw a drop of cum began to squirt out. He put his dick in my mouth, and he jerked the rest into my mouth.

"That's a good nigger girl. Now, let me see you swallow it all."

I swallowed, and I almost threw up on his Casper looking legs.

"That's protein for you," he said as he got dressed. He smiled and said, "I will see you at the same time tomorrow, nigger bitch."

When he left, I stuck my finger in the middle of my throat. I saved my vomit mixed with his sperm in a cup under the bed. He wasn't going to get away with this. I had his DNA in a cup. I was going to report him to someone, but who? I stood up and looked at the picture of Dr. Martin Luther King Jr., and I began to pray. I removed the darts from his eyes. I put my hand on his face. I didn't know much about him, but I knew he had marched for my rights. Mama had this same picture of him in our front room on the wall. This actually looks like the same picture.

This went on for about two weeks, and, each time, he would confide in me and talk about his family. I had fourteen cups of his sperm mixed with my vomit under the bed. The smell was awful. It made me sick to my stomach. He didn't even say anything about the smell. He'd say, "You need a bath, nigger girl."

When it was time for me to be released from the hole, Ms. Allgood came and got me.

"What is that awful smell?" she said as she opened the door.

"It's this," I said as I started to pull the cups from under the bed.

"What the fuck are those?" she asked, holding her nose.

"This is my vomit and Mr. Knox's sperm. He made me suck his dick, and we have to report him to the warden. I threw up this, and this is my evidence."

"Bitch, are you crazy?" she said as she went to look for a janitor in the hallway.

"No, I'm not crazy! Look at these red marks around my neck. He has to be stopped! Ms. Allgood, please say something. You're not going to let him get away with this, are you? All he talks about is how much he hate blacks. Look at this picture," I said as I went to go point at Dr. Martin Luther King Jr, but there was now a picture of Ronald Reagan where Dr. King's picture had been.

"What?" I asked, stunned. "There was a picture of him right here, and he was playing darts with his face. Where did the picture go?"

"Hallucinations usually happens when you're down here for more than seven days. You've been down here for fourteen days, and you're starting to hallucinate. That's normal, but we have medicine for girls like you."

"I'm not crazy! This nasty shit has his sperm mixed in it."

"If you say one more thing about that nasty mix, I will make you drink them all."

She called a janitor in to clean the room and discard my evidence. I was shit out of luck.

13
Back in Population

When we headed back upstairs, all the girls didn't clap. They had looks of sympathy on their faces. They must have all known that I was down in Mr. Knox's hell hole. Sticky Fingers even had a surprised look on her face when I got to our cell.

There was something different about her. She had cut her cornrows off. She really looked like a boy. She had a low haircut, and she had gotten tattoos on both of her shoulders. As she stood there, looking at herself in the mirror, I laid on my bunk, face down. I was exhausted. I was terrified, and now I was back in the cell with my enemy. I didn't want to say anything to her. I wasn't going to be a friend of hers nor was I going to give her my pussy. *The room is different*, I thought as I turned over on my back and looked around. She had more posters on the wall. She even had a surround sound system in there. She even decorated the cell door with signs that read I RUN THIS MOTHERFUCKER! I couldn't believe what my eyes were seeing. There had to be someone that could do something about these hell raisers in here.

"I can't wait to hear what you have to say in discussion time," she said as she joined me on my bed.

"Can you please get off of my bunk?"

"I can sleep on this bunk with you if I want to," she said as she acted like she was about to lie down.

I looked her in her face, and I saw straight through her. She was trying to get me in trouble again, but I was not falling for her stupid mind games.

"So, are you going to talk about that racist ass Mr. Knox's hell hole? Every girl that has went down there has come back up and had to take meds for the rest of their lives or they took their own lives. So, did you have fun sucking his skinny, white pencil pecker? Did you enjoy looking at those green veins that ran through his pale white thighs? Did you enjoy calling him master when he fucked you in the asshole? Did you get mad when he told you to get on your black nigger knees? Did you like being called the word nigger from a R. Lee Emery-looking motherfucker?"

I had no choice but to give in to Sticky Fingers because I wasn't about to let her get under my skin. If I would have hit her, I would have gotten hauled off to Mr. Knox's hell hole again, while she remained free in population. I thought about it for a minute as I took in everything that she had just said. I rubbed my feet against her arm and said, "When do you want me?"

"What?" she said as she cleared her throat.

"You're so used to taking pussy. Now, I am asking you when do you want to make love to me?"

She got up and walked to the corner and grabbed and comforter and hung it over the cell door.

"I can fuck you right now," she said as she made sure the comforter was sturdy.

"Not right now. You know all of the things that go on in Mr. Knox's hell hole. So, I'll tell you what. First, I'm going to take a shower and freshen up for you."

She moved the comforter back and opened the cell door.

"Make sure you wash good in between those lips because I don't want to smell anything," she said as I left.

When I walked out and got to the shower area, they were all taken. Then, I remembered that we had to pair up and take showers together. I went to the shower on the end that only had one set of feet in it. When I opened up the shower curtain, I saw Crystal. She was just standing there, letting water run down her face. I looked at her back. It was covered with red whelps.

"Who did this to you?" I asked as I entered the shower. "Did Mr. Knox do this to you?"

I tried to comfort her.

"Please don't touch me. I am sore all over," she said as she made room for me to join her. "I don't think I can live like this in here. I am going to do it tonight."

"Do what tonight?" I asked as I grabbed the V05 shampoo.

"I'm going to take my own life. The Bible says that God has many mansions, and I want to go live with Him. This is hell! Don't you see?" she said as she faced me with more whelps on her chest and breasts. "It says in the book John that God has prepared a place for us."

"Can you please tell me who did this to you?"

"It doesn't matter who did this to me. Nothing will be done! We're in the middle of nowhere, and the Bible is the only thing that helps me in here. If I knew I was going to get treated like this, I would have let Ray continue to rape me."

"Don't say that," I said as I gently held her close. "Don't say that. I will figure something out. You did right. He should have died, but please don't take your own life. I think I have a plan that will help us."

"Please tell me because I am going to God's mansion soon. I am so eager to get there."

"No! Wait before you do that. I think, if you kill yourself, you will go to Hell." "No, but the Bible said that God went to go and prepare a place."

"Well, that may be true, but look for the part where it

talks about taking your own life. Crystal, I am going to give into Sticky Fingers, and I'm going to trick her into believing that I really like her, so, that way, we'll have more freedom. You know we have to butter them up. It seems that she has had every girl in here except me. And I will not go to that hole another day if I can help it."

"Yep, you're right she has had us all. She even had me with Kenya at the same time."

"We have to stop being so defensive. We have to act like the things that they say to us don't bother us. We have to just ignore them. Life isn't fair to some, but killing yourself will only make things worse. So, this is the plan. I will become one of Sticky's girls, and I will play her. I will find out all the dirt that she has on Ms. Allgood, and I will use it to my advantage."

"But how are you going to do that?"

"I don't know, but, at least, I have a start. I will cross that bridge when I get to it. Look at me and promise me that you won't kill yourself?"

"I can't promise you that I won't kill myself, but I can promise you that it won't be tonight."

14
Sticky Fingers

When I got back to our cell, Sticky Fingers had lit candles and had some soft music playing. I looked on my bed, and she had laid out some Victoria's Secret lingerie.

"Where did you get this?" I asked as I towel dried my hair.

"I have my resources," she said as she walked over and led me to my bunk. "I bet you'll look real good in this."

She held it up and put it up against my skin. "Red is looking good on you already, and you don't even have it on. Do you remember when I said that I wanted you to dance for me?"

"Yes. I remember. You want me to be your nasty dancer."

"Wow! You remembered the song and everything."

She walked over to her CD player and put in Kilo's "Nasty Dancer".

"I know you have a little white in you, so I hope that your black side knows how to dance."

I sat on my bunk and undressed. Then, I put on the sleek lingerie. It fit good around the waist, but the breast part was too big.

"Oh, don't worry about the breast part. My last bitch wore this, and she had bigger breasts than you. You look so pretty," she said as she fired up a cigarette. "You don't have to worry about being my girl for long. I just want to be able to say that I've fucked every girl that has stepped foot in this facility. This has to make me tough for the big house."

Taking pussy will not make you a bully in prison, I thought.

"But what if I want to be your girl for a long time? What if I want you to protect me from Ms. Allgood and that racist ass Mr. Knox?"

"No one has ever wanted to be my main chick. I guess I could be your man," she said as she poured herself a cup of wine.

"Let me guess. You have your resources for the wine, too."

"Yep," she said as she handed me a cup.

I needed something stronger to get me through this deal that I had just made with the devil.

"Stand up and let me watch you shake those thick thighs."

I don't know what she was looking at because I was skin and bones. I wasn't eating that food, and I had lost so much weight. I stood up and took a sip of the wine and began to dance. I pushed her into the chair and began to dance for her like Demi did for Burt Reynolds in Striptease.

"I like that," she said as she took off her bandanna. "I like to be physical when I have sex."

She took another sip of wine. I looked at myself in the mirror as I danced, and I thought to myself, *At least, I look cute doing this.* My hair had dried up, and it was naturally curly. It was brown and blonde. She rubbed my thighs as I danced on her lap.

"Pour me some more wine," I said as I shook my breasts in her face.

"You shouldn't have played so hard to get in the first place," she said as she got up to pour me another cup.

"I wasn't playing hard to get. I was just waiting on the right time," I said as I threw her back in the chair.

"So, you're saying that you were going to give in all along?"

"Yep," I said as I bent over to shake my ass in her face.

"Oh, you have a pretty pussy! I can't wait to taste that."

"I can't wait for you to taste it either," I whispered in her ear.

"I am getting aroused just by you dancing."

"I am, too, so what do you want to do next?"

"I want to fuck you."

I walked to my bunk slowly and laid down. She took off her t-shirt. Underneath, she had on a wife beater. I saw that she had taped down her breasts. I laid on my back and opened my legs. She went and grabbed a dildo and said, "I'll be gentle."

I wasn't scared, but I was nervous. This was my first time ever having sex, and it was with a girl! Never in a million years did I picture my life like this. She licked her two middle fingers and rubbed them against my clit.

"Have you ever came before?" she asked as she continued to rub my clit.

"Have I ever what? No, I haven't. What does that mean?" I said as I opened my legs wider for her to get a better feel.

"It's the feeling you get when you have an orgasm."

"A what?"

I was completely lost. All I knew was that her fingers were making me feel good. No one had never played with my pussy before, not even me! I was feeling an indescribable feeling that was beginning to make my body tingle. She was moving her fingers rapidly across my clit and licking on my earlobe at the same time.

"You see. That feeling you're getting ready to feel means you're about to cum," she whispered. She stopped and made her way down between my legs. Her tongue was so fat, and she licked my whole pussy in one stroke. Her tongue was warm, and I felt her sliding her fingers in and out of my pussy. I was praying that the feeling came soon because I felt her saliva running between my asshole. I didn't like that feeling, just the thought of knowing that it was her spit down there.

"How does that feel?" she asked as she came up for air.

"It feels good," I said as I pushed her head back down. "Don't ever stop when I'm about to cum."

She licked, and I finally came in her mouth. She stuck her fingers in my pussy and showed me my cum on her fingers. It was clear and slimy.

"That was a good feeling," I said as I sat up in the bed.

"We're not finished. I have to fuck you. I only ate you out. Now, you have to feel the power of this," she said as she held up a dildo that was connected to a belt.

She put the dildo around her waist. And she looked just like a boy. I laid back down and closed my eyes. She kissed me on my neck. Then, she eased her tongue in my mouth. We were kissing, and I felt something in her mouth. It was my pussy hair.

"Can you please go gargle with some mouthwash?"

"You can't stand the taste of your own pussy."

"No. It's not that. You have my pussy hair in your mouth."

She got up and turned up the bottle of wine and said, "There. It's washed down with the rest of them."

I almost threw up at the thought of pussy hairs sliding

down her throat with wine. "Now, where were we?" she said as she came back to the bunk.

"You were about to pass me the bottle of wine."

She looked so funny with that dildo moving every time she walked. I turned up the bottle, and I only left a drop in there. She got on top of me, and she slid the dildo in my soaking wet pussy.

"Am I hurting you?" she asked as she eased it in some more.

"No. You're fine," I said as I slid my tongue in her mouth.

I didn't want to do this, but I had to do what I had to do. She was on top me, stroking to the beat of Keith Sweat's song "Right and a Wrong Way". I was so into it that I didn't notice that she had changed the music from fast to slow. I didn't feel my pussy pop. I remember when I was in school all the boys used to ask the girls if they'd had their cherry popped. Although it felt like the plastic was cutting me, I didn't do anything but just lie there imagining that she was J.J. I focused on her tattoos. They were the only thing that made her look like a boy because her face was very feminine. She had thick eyebrows and long eyelashes. And her skin tone was brown skinned. I rubbed her back as if she was J.J. After a few more pumps, she had stopped and said that she was tired. I knew she was going to get tired sooner or later because she wasn't getting any stimulation. She laid next to me, and I turned over and started to rub her waves in the top of her head.

"If you keep fucking and eating me out like this, I will fall in love with you. I never came before, and that was a great feeling."

"I thought you were just bullshitting. You really were a virgin?"

"Yes, I was. One thing you will learn about me is I don't lie. I learned not to tell lies because, when you do, you have to remember the first lie that you told in the first place. And you have to think of another one to cover the one you just told. Lying leads to nowhere. I want to be honest with you, and I want you to be honest with me. Can you do that, Sticky?"

"Well, that all depends on what you want me to be honest about."

"Why did Ms. Allgood whip Crystal on her back like she was a white slave?"

"Girl, is that what she told you?" she said as she sat up in the bed and looked at me.

"Well, not exactly, but someone did it to her, and that just doesn't sit too well with me."

"Mr. Knox did it that to her because she refused to swallow his sperm."

"Have you swallowed his sperm? I reluctantly asked.

"Hell, no! Regina...I mean Ms. Allgood wouldn't have that shit happen to me!"

"Who's Regina?"

"Nobody," she nervously said as she took the comforter off of the cell door.

She looked at me and said, "We're about to have some company."

I quickly jumped up and put back on my YDC uniform. It was the warden and Ms. Allgood.

"Count time!" I heard her shout.

Sticky just stood there in her wife beater. I jumped up and headed for the door. She looked in on us and kept walking. The warden followed closely behind her with a notepad. I wanted to tell her what had happened to me in the hole, but she probably wouldn't do anything. Besides, she was in agreement with Ms. Allgood when she told everyone that she was the H.N.I.C.

"Come on. Let's finish talking," I said as I went back to my bunk.

"We can talk later tonight. All that fucking has worked up an appetite."

She was the only girl who could go and come as she pleased. She was the only girl that could order from the store. She was the only girl that had the resources to get special shit. I was going to find out who her resources were even if it killed me.

15
Tattle Tail

While Sticky was out of the cell doing only God knows what, Ms. Allgood came in the cell. She looked around and said, "You look like you've been having fun in here. I see you decided to get along with Retina... I mean Sticky... after all."

"Ms. Allgood, it doesn't bother you that one of your colleagues is racist? Did you know that he was calling me nigger bitch for the whole two weeks that I was in the hole? What is this place? Is this place even legal?"

"You shut up right now, or I will shut you up. You're asking too many questions, and we have medicine for little girls like you."

I realized that she was serious about the medicine because she reached in her pocket and pulled out a few capsules.

"I'm sorry. I will just mind my business. I am on your list, and I am getting along with Sticky, so there's no way I could get thrown back in the hole because I got along with everybody else."

"Well, you keep it that way," she said as she left.

I drifted off to sleep, and I was awakened by a commotion outside of the cell. It was a fight going on between Sticky and Jennifer. *The teacher's pet and the teacher's slut are fighting*, I thought. At first, I was going to break it up, but I didn't want to get snatched up and get thrown in the hole. *What could these two possibly be fighting about?* She was getting the best of Sticky which I so enjoyed, but then I remembered that I needed Sticky to believe that I was down for her, so I decided to get in the squabble. I grabbed Jennifer by her hair, and, just as I was about to smack her in her face, I felt a cold hand grab my wrist. It was Mr. Knox, and I just knew that Sticky was going to stick up for me and tell him that this wasn't my fight.

"I see you like Mr. Knox's hell hole," he said as he dragged me down the hall.

"No! Please! No! Please!" I begged as I scratched the floor, trying to hold on for dear life. All of the girls were quiet as they looked on and watched me being dragged down the hall defenselessly.

"I got something for you, nigger bitch," he said as he switched hands to get a firmer grip on my hair. I was scratching the floor, screaming, "Please don't make me go! Please don't make me go!"

He didn't listen to me as I begged and cried. He threw me in the cell and said, "I will be back in five minutes."

He slammed the door shut. I looked around the satanic hole, and, sure enough, the Dr. King picture was hung up as a dart game. He had colored his eyes red, and he had five darts in his teeth lined up as a smile. He was a racist son of a bitch, and I had it in my heart to kill him. The way he had called me a nigger bitch just made me want to see him beg for his life. *I could actually watch him beg.* I wouldn't even feel sorry for him. I got on my knees and prayed, "God, I know you hear me. How can you watch this man continue to do such horrible things to me and to all of the other girls for that matter? Is there any truth to that Bible? The words that Jesus spoke in red, can I believe them? God, I need to know that you are in real? I need to know that you, in fact, exist? God, please touch Mr. Knox's heart and let him have a change of heart. Please let him come in here and be a different man.

God, please let my good behavior release date be coming soon? You've watched me, God, and you've seen that I am not the troublemaker here. In Jesus' name, I pray. Amen."

As I stood up, I heard keys jingling at the door. My heart started beating rapidly. He walked in and looked at me again for about five minutes. Then, he slapped me with the back of his hand and said, "You had evidence, you filthy nigger whore! Didn't I tell you that the blacks in here aren't on your side either? We destroyed your cups of evidence. Do you know how many nigger bitches that come here don't leave here alive? Would you like the make the fiftieth one? For some reason, you black bitches don't seem to hear very well."

He unbuckled his pants. Then, he said, "I used to fuck this nigger bitch in a country town, but I had to kill her. She was talking crazy, saying things like she had a surprise for me, but, when I got there, I didn't like her surprise. I surprised her. I killed her nigger ass, but, in here, it's different. All of you nigger bitches in here seem to kill your damn selves, which is fine by me because no one loves you and no one will miss you."

I listened to him, and I saw the game that he was trying to play. He was trying to get me mentally fucked up in my head, but I didn't say anything. I just stood there, trembling like a leaf on the ground.

"Can you believe that my great-grandparents were nigger owners? I've even had some of your kind to call me 'master' in here. That's what I think I'll have you call me while I'm fucking you in your asshole. And I dare you to shit out that evidence and try to keep that! Now, this time, I will have you down here for a month, and I can make you my little nigger slave. Would you like that?" he said. His face was just one inch from mine.

"Yes, sir. I would," I said, looking him in his evil amber green eyes.

"You know, if my wife took it in the ass, I wouldn't fuck you girls in yours, but I enjoy watching your ass shake like jelly. If Maria did take it in the ass, it wouldn't shake at all."

I stood up and took off of my clothes without him ordering me to. I laid on the bed and opened my legs up. My heart was crying, but I wasn't going to let the tears roll down my face. He got on top of me, trying to get his dick hard. He then got up and grabbed a *Playboy* magazine. He opened it up and put it on my face.

"I will not look at you," he said as he shoved his dick into my pussy. "Miss December, your white ass looks so fine."

He humped me about eight to ten times. Then, he told me to turn over, and I felt him put the magazine in the middle of my back. He spit on my ass. Then, he rubbed his dick in his spit and shoved it in my ass. I put a hump in my back, making the magazine fall. He elbowed me in my back and ordered me to be still.

"See what you made me do?" he said as he humped me harder. "Call me master."

He slapped me on my ass and yelled, "Call me master!"

"Master," I mumbled as I tried to sniff the snot that was coming out of my nose. I didn't want him to know that I was crying.

"Louder, nigger bitch! Do you want another elbow to the kidneys?"

"Master!" I yelled as I took the pain from him fucking me in my ass. "Fuck me in my ass, master! Fuck me harder, master!"

I was looking at Dr. King's picture, reflecting on his "I Have a Dream" speech.

"I'm about to come in your nigger asshole. Would you like that, nigger bitch?"

"Yes, master. Please fill my nigger asshole up. Please! Is that all you got? Fuck me harder, master!"

"Keep talking to me like that," he said as he was about to reach his peak.

I felt his sweat dripping on my back as he fucked me harder and harder. He finally stopped and pushed me on the floor. I slid back into the corner on the cold floor. I looked at Dr. King's picture again.

"That nigger can't save you. Can you believe he marched for y'all dumb niggers to vote and y'all don't even do that? If you ask me, he died for nothing because y'all niggers are still pulling triggers, killing one another. Y'all's history was fucked up then, and it's still fucked up in the new millennium. Y'all blacks will never learn. Some of y'all are so stupid that you really want Ebonics in the dictionary. Those are nigger words that y'all's nigger asses made up because y'all can't pronounce correct English. I will be back in here to bring you some supper," he said as he put on his clothes and left.

16
Why Confide in Me?

I had been in the hole so many days that I eventually lost count. I didn't know the time of day. I knew I'd been down there longer than a month. Mr. Knox was still doing the same shit, but he was starting to talk about his family more. I didn't want to hear any of his bullshit, but the more I listened to him the more I realized that he was just a miserable, old man. His daughter had run off with a Meth addict, his son was gay, and his wife refused to have sex with him, but I still didn't see why he took all his frustrations out on us. We were just there to do our time. It was almost time for me to get out, and I was hoping that Ms. Allgood or the warden would come and save me.

Strangely, I was eating really good while I was down there. I was eating steaks and potatoes. The more I called him master, the better I ate. I had gotten my weight back up, and I was a little thicker. My hair had grown so long that it was almost to my butt. He stopped fucking me with the magazines. Now, he was calling me Maria, his wife's name.

Time moved so slow in there. All I could do was throw water on my face and exercise to keep my sanity. These walls talked to me sometimes. There were days when I thought I was going to lose my mind. I even thought about taking my own life, but I believed in God, and I knew I would be on top in the end. It was so quiet in there that you could hear a mouse taking a shit.

I was no longer a virgin. I had been violated from head to toe. It didn't count with Sticky, but Mr. Knox made sure that he fucked me in every hole that was available on my body. We were living in the hole like I was Maria for real. He would come in and tell me what was going on with the girls upstairs. He told me that Sticky Fingers had gotten another girlfriend. I didn't care. I was relieved. He also told me that Crystal had killed herself. I was sad at first, but I would have probably kill myself, too, if I had let this place get the best of me. Now, she was burning in hell for sure. I had specifically told her that, if she killed herself, she would go straight to hell. He told me that, once I left the hole with him, I was getting on a bus, and I would be going home. I was so happy, and I wasn't too fond of him telling me his fucked up life, but I had no choice but to listen.

"Why didn't you kill me?" I asked as I opened up a sparkling can of Dr. Pepper.

"You are an important asset," he said as he stood up and threw a dart at Dr. King's picture. "You have ties to Spyder."

He smiled, showing his tobacco coated teeth.

"Spyder?" I said as I almost choked on the soda.

"You see, darling. Word around town is he has millions in his safe, and I would look very suspicious snooping around there. That's where you come in at? You see. I don't make much money in here with you miserable nigger bitches, so I figured, if you could help me get my paws on those unmarked bills, I could finally leave that ugly-ass wife of mine and be on another continent drinking whisky. Now, I have arranged for you to get out early. All you have to do is follow my plan."

"Can you at least give me one million?"

"Hell, no, nigger bitch! Your probation officer is a good friend of mine. You will get a job and work for a living."

All I could think was, *If I get my hands on that cash, J.J and I are going to leave town.*

17
Free at Last

"Rise and shine," he said as he opened the door.

He walked in, carrying a tray with bacon, eggs, grits, and toast. It smelled so good.

"After you finish this delicious breakfast with this freshly squeezed orange juice, I want to get one last nut. I want to fuck that nigger pussy one last time before you go out in the free world."

There was something so familiar about his amber green eyes. Could he have been one of mama's men at the house? I didn't remember seeing a white man, but, half of the time, when she had company, I would only see them when they were leaving.

It was my release day, and I wanted to buck and say no, but that would only make things worse. He did say that he had killed before, and I didn't want to take any chances. There was definitely something about his eyes that made me not fear him anymore. There was something about him that made me want to just give in. The feelings that I had for him were weird. One minute, I wanted him dead, and the next I wanted to look into his amber green eyes, reaching the peak of his soul.

"What took you so long?" I asked as I took a sip of my orange juice to wash down the thick grits.

It had been three days since I'd seen him. I was getting used to him coming to the hell hole every night, gossiping to me about the drama that went on upstairs. He looked at me and said, "Niggers don't get to ask questions. I was with my family. I do have somewhat of a life outside of this place."

I didn't care what he did outside of this place. I was going to go to the president if I had to. Not only had he humiliated and violated me from head to toe, he was blackmailing me as well. If I got my hands on the millions in Spyder's safe, I was going to go AWOL. I wasn't going to care about any probation or anything. *Money can buy a lot*, I thought as I daydreamed about what life would be like in the arms of J.J.

After being in the hell hole with Mr. Knox, I realized that he only wanted someone to talk to. He couldn't bond with his son because he was gay. He said that his wife didn't listen to him anymore. He said that she had even cut their sex life off. He even told me that he had dated a black chick named Lynette. I don't know why he told me so much of his personal life, but he did. Some days, he would come to the hole pissed, and, of course, those were the days when I had to call him *master*.

After I finished eating my breakfast, he threw the tray on the floor. He didn't throw me on the bed like he usually did before we had sex. He sat in the chair and said that he wanted me to ride him. I sat on his dick. He unbuttoned my shirt as I was putting his dick in my pussy. He licked my breasts and pulled my hair at the same time. I was getting a headache, and I wasn't amused about by getting my hair pulled. The harder I rode him, the harder he pulled my hair. I was trying to fuck him fast, so he would hurry up and cum. Just as he was about to cum, he threw me on the floor and stood over me and squeezed his hot sperm all over my chest.

"You won't have a mixed breed nigger baby with me," he said as he continued to release his semen. "Ah, that feels like a breath of fresh air. You can take a shower and get ready to leave. Today is your lucky day. I just might take you upstairs, so you can say your good-byes to those other mentally ill bitches. I couldn't think of who I wanted to say good bye to. The only friend I'd had was Crystal, and she was dead. I had wanted to befriend Kenya, but she was not the friendly type. She was twisted, and she didn't want to talk to anyone. I didn't give a fuck about saying good bye to Sticky Fingers or Ms. Allgood.

I took a shower to try and get his scent off of me. I stood in there and just let the hot water damn near burn my skin, but the water wasn't hot enough to get his memories off of me. As I stood in the shower, I reminisced about Mama and her "get out" fits. I recalled one time when she looked at me and said, "You have devil eyes just like him, and I don't trust you." I never knew what she meant. I never knew who *he* was. I wished that she was alive to put me out one last time. I would have made sure that I told her that I loved her. I had so many unanswered questions floating in my head. I wanted to ask her who my father was. I wanted to ask her who her mother was, but I guess those were questions that I would never find the answers to. I began to tear up because of the way she had died. Whoever killed her didn't have any sympathy for her. From what J.J had told me, she didn't have a chance. He told me that someone had crept in the back door and attacked Mama while she was passed out on the sofa drunk. Who would take the time to slit a person's neck? Then, laughter came upon my face because I remembered a time when Mama and I were at the corner store. She had made a bet with me and said that she would race me to the house. In all fairness, I was younger than her and I knew would beat her, but I slowed up for her to win. She ran as fast as she could with her brown bag of beer and cigarettes.

"I'm closing in on you," I would say as I continued to slow my pace for her to win. She ran into the house and collapsed on the sofa. She said, "Tasha Jean girl, you got me tired."

And I said, "Lie back, Mama, and rest your feet."

18
Fuck this Mental Ward

I got out the shower and found Mr. Knox standing there, looking at me with a mouth full of tobacco.

"You know I am really counting on your black ass to get that money for me out of Spyder's safe," he said as he spit in the silver garbage pail.

I looked at him as I dried my hair and said, "You made it possible for me to get out of this hell hole two years early. I will do whatever you need me to do. I am your girl."

"Another thing. When your black ass gets out, you have to keep quiet about us. I'm a respected citizen in my community. Once I get my hands on those unmarked bills, I will be set for life. I can leave and not ever worry about you mentally challenged bitches ever again. I've been on this job for twenty-five years, and I will not let a cunt like you take me down."

I shook my head like I was agreeing with him. I had a plan that would exploit his ass and this crazy ass YDC facility. *It is only a matter of time. This white cop has fucked with the wrong little black girl.* I was glad to go home early. I would be finally able to hug and kiss J.J. all over.

"You get dressed, and I will be back in five minutes to take you to say your good-byes to the other twisted bitches."

I was glad when he left the room. I looked under the bed, and there was a notebook under there. I zipped it up in my uniform as I put it on. I was leaving this place, and I didn't want any memories of this place, but, if I could take the letters that the girls had written to the president, then maybe they could shut this place down. Hopefully, they would lock their asses up, too. They were the real criminals. They were abusers and child molesters. Ms. Allgood was killing her own kind in there, and Mr. Knox don't give a fuck if you were black or white. Look at what happened to Crystal. She was white, and he whipped her back like she was a black slave. It wasn't about race in this place. It was simply about power. And they definitely had the power over us troubled girls. I looked further under the bed, and I saw the Dr. King picture that Mr. Knox used as a dart game, I picked it up, and an envelope fell out. I heard the keys jingling on Mr. Knox's waist as I stuffed the envelope in my pocket.

"There has been a change of plans," he said as he opened the door. "Apparently, there has been some type of delay with the bus that is supposed to take you back home."

I thought he was going to tell me that I wasn't being released after all.

"So, what now master?"

"You can go back upstairs and join them for that discussion bullshit or you can suck on my pecker."

"I will take option one please."

"Niggers don't have options, but, since we have new niggers coming in, I won't need you anymore."

We walked upstairs and I walked in on Jennifer. She was singing a song called "Two Wrongs Does Make it Right".

Verse 1
Whoever said two wrongs don't make it right is a lie
Two wrongs does make it right and I'm going to tell you why
I put in work being there for my man day and night
And he gets up and walks out after a childish fight

Leaving me is not what I'm pissed off about
He left me for my best friend and I found out
She had the nerve to call me and sound all cool
When all along, they both had been playing me for a fool
Chorus:
Two wrongs does make it right and all it took was one childish fight
You wanted to leave me all alone
You just needed an excuse to leave home
I'm not going to break down and cry
Even though this relationship to you has been one big lie

Verse 2
So I decided to go out and clear my mind
And I ran into your homeboy who is so damn fine
Just like you've been giving her the eye at our cook-outs
I've been sleeping with him and Jr. was "our look-out"
Yes, Jr. your son that I pushed out
Now, how do you feel with that being out?
I'm tired of being so damn nice and oh so sweet
My other personality you're about to meet
So they ask me how could I do a good man like that
But they didn't know that you were a cheater dressed in black
You really thought that you were slick but I was ten steps ahead
I had your best friend first, and guess what? It was in our bed.
It might sound dirty and low down
But I had him as a sidekick because you were never around.

Chorus
Two wrongs does make it right and all it took was one childish fight
You wanted to leave me all alone
You just needed an excuse to leave home
I'm not going to break down and cry
Even though this relationship to you has been one big lie

"Don't clap just yet," she said as she flipped over the paper to sing another song. "This song is dedicated to the man we all know as Jesus. This song is called 'Him'."

She had a beautiful voice, and, to me, she sounded like she could sing gospel as well.

Verse 1
I didn't need all the drugs to numb the pain
All I needed was HIM in those times of shame
All I had to do was fall on my knees and call his name
Instead of looking for someone to blame
All the bad I've done, it's too late to take back
Not to mention the drugs that could have given me a heart attack
If I can come from where I came from
I'm in my prime and there is so much more to come
He loves me and this I know
And NO the bible isn't the only thing that told me so
I've been through Hell and back
And it was HIM who had my back

Chorus
Ever since I found HIM
He's been such a joy
I was just like a kid playing with a brand new toy
Having HIM is such a relief and that I did find out
And he's never left my side without a doubt

Verse 2
I thought I was supposed to do drugs and drink everyday
Because my ancestors had paved the way
It was a generational curse
And every month it was damn near another hearse

We didn't try to do things to change the past
All we wanted was a high that would last
I'm still going through it, and I am seeing things so clear
I really want my health to get better this year
I got so tired of playing the name game
I had to get on my knees and scream out his name
Jesus, please help me! Can't you see that I need you right now?
I want to get closer to you. Please just show me how.

Chorus
Ever since I found HIM
He's been such a joy
I was just like a kid playing with a brand new toy
Having him was such a relief and that I did find out
And he's never left my side without a doubt

    I was crying when she got done, and all the girls wanted her to sing more. I didn't mind listening to her, especially since she had such a good voice. She could hit the high notes, and she knew just when to tone them down, and she was singing them songs acapella!
    "More! More! More!" they shouted.
    "Are you guys really feeling me?" she said as she unfolded another piece of paper. "Well, if you guys, insist here's one more. This song is called 'I Cheated'.

Verse 1
Baby, take a seat. I have something to say
These words that I have to say should have come out yesterday
I've got to say this and get this off of my chest
But let me take a drink before I tell you the rest
Remember last week when I had that stain on my dress
I got it from another man that I was trying to impress

Chorus
I cheated and I should have never started
But if I break it off we'll all be broken hearted
I knew all of the times when you were with her
But I didn't want to picture it, so I kept it in my mind as a blur
I'm cheating with him and it feels so right
Especially when he goes deep and holds me tight

Verse 2
We were only supposed to talk and exchange a few words
I know all of this sounds absurd
Sweetheart you make love to me good. You really, really do
But when I know you're with her I don't know what to do
I need to be held like a baby all through the day
Now I feel like a bitch that has gone astray
Now baby hold on before you say that I'm wrong
I knew all about you bringing her to our home
When you're with me you're thinking of her
So I found me a decent man that I prefer
He tells me that his wife is cheating on him too
And the man she's doing it with is you

Chorus
I cheated and I should have never started
But if I break it off we'll all be broken hearted
I knew all of the times when you were with her
But I didn't want to picture it, so I kept it in my mind as a blur
I'm cheating with him and it feels so right
Especially when he goes deep and hold me tight

Verse 3

I didn't want to cheat on you the very first time
But your unfaithfulness was on my mind
When I caught you, I quickly forgave you
But I felt betrayed and I wanted to get revenge back at you
You said that you didn't have a problem with my weight
But that was a lie, and I've taken just about all I can take
I see how you look at other women when we go out
But I'm your fucking wife, so what's that shit all about.

19
Singing-ass Jennifer

Everyone was so moved by her songs. The girls beat on the tables, so she could have a beat for her songs. I kept looking at the clock, I was ready to go and see J.J.
I couldn't believe that there was a delay in the bus, but what could I do? It could be worse. I could be down in the hell hole screaming master. I looked around at the girls and saw that Sticky Fingers was the main one beating on the tables. I was in the hole because of them two. Now, she was chanting her on like they were the best of friends. This place had really taught me a valuable lesson. And that was not to trust any one! Jennifer looked over at Ms. Allgood and winked her eye. Just the thought of those two having sex made my stomach turn. Ms. Allgood looked like she had three stomachs.

"Sing all you want," Ms. Allgood said as she blew her a kiss.

"I am so glad you guys really like my songs. I will probably make it in the real world once I get out. I will sing three more. Then, I will sit down and let someone else come up here. This song is called 'Color Blind.'"

Song 1

Chorus
I was color blind at first by your green
But I found out the grass wasn't so green
So I took it upon myself to go to school and get some skills
Because I wanted to be independent and pay my own bills

You had all the money and it's not so funny
When I make my own money, you'll be the one looking like a dummy

Verse 1
You got money and you think that you can talk to me any kind of way
But I pray to God that I will be able to leave your ass one day
I tried to stay in it for our kids' sake
But leaving you and your ego was a piece of cake
I can't lie. I got caught up and relaxed in the fame
But you treat me like trash in public and that's a damn shame

Chorus
I was color blind at first by your green
But I found out the grass wasn't so green
So I took it upon myself to go to school and get some skills
Because I want to be independent and pay my own bills
You had all the money and it's not so funny
When I make my own money, you'll be the one looking like a dummy

Verse 2
So go ahead and keep the money, cars, the house, and plus the clothes
I'm tired of catching you with different hoes
I was so stupid and too damn blind to see
That your heart was never meant for me
I was your lady until you started acting shady
Now I have more money than you, and I'm such a lady
So I know you're just about to go broke
And when you had me you shouldn't have taken me for a joke

Chorus
I was colored blind at first by your green
But I found out the grass wasn't so green

So I took it upon myself to go to school and get some skills
Because I want to be independent and pay my own bills
You had all the money and it's not so funny
When I make my own money, you'll be the one looking like a dummy

Song 2

"Teddy Bear"

Chorus
I'm sleeping with my teddy bear can't you see
I'm sleeping with him because he comforts me
He listens to me and plus he's so soft
I hate it when you ignore me when I'm at your loft
Yes, you ignore me but teddy makes me feel so free
But if he came to life that would be a sight to see
He respects my mind body and my soul
His heart for me will never turn cold

Verse 1
Boy you never listen to me
Now I'm with teddy and he feels so good to me
He knows when to hush up the fuss
He's not like you he'll never curse
Teddy has the cutest big black eyes
And he's always quiet never telling lies
I never have to worry about teddy being gone
Because he's always in my bed when I get home

Chorus
I'm sleeping with my teddy bear can't you see
I'm sleeping with him because he comforts me

He listens to me and plus he's so soft
I hate it when you ignore me when I'm at your loft
Yes, you ignore me but teddy makes me feel so free
But if he came to life that would be a sight to see
He respects my mind body and my soul
His heart for me will never turn cold

Verse 2
You're welcomed to come back in my life
If you're willing to change and make me your wife
I want you to be the man I first knew
But you've changed so much and I haven't got a clue

Chorus
I'm sleeping with my teddy bear can't you see
I'm sleeping with him because he comforts me
He listens to me and plus he's so soft
I hate it when you ignore me when I'm at your loft
Yes, you ignore me but teddy makes me feel so free
But if he came to life that would be a sight to see
He respects my mind body and my soul
His heart for me will never turn cold

Song 3
Tip of the Iceberg

Chorus
You're at the tip of the iceberg at the very top
And the love that I have for you is about to stop
When we're out, your eyes are wondering, looking at him and her
Hell I can't figure out which sex you prefer

Verse 1

White Cop, Lil Black Gurl

You're on the down low and you're undercover
I've seen you with several other brothers
I'm sick of going through this shit with you
All of this hard work and effort that I put into you
There is somebody for everybody and this is so true
I just hate I put my heart and soul all into you

Chorus
You're at the tip of the iceberg at the very top
And the love that I have for you is about to stop
When we're out your eyes are wondering, looking at him and her
Hell I can't figure out which sex you prefer

Verse 2
You have your days when you make me feel good
But then you make me sad when you come home mad
When we had that foursome I knew right then
That you were looking at him more than his girlfriend

Chorus
You're at the tip of the iceberg at the very top
And the love that I have for you is about to stop
When we're out your eyes are wondering, looking at him and her
Hell I can't figure out which sex you prefer

20
The Devil with Green Eyes

"May I go up next please? I have something to say." I asked, raising my hand.

"I don't see why not. This is your last day," Ms. Allgood said.

As I walked up, I saw Mr. Knox out the corner of my eye.

"I want to just share something with you guys that has been heavy on my heart. I want to ask God questions like why my life? What did I do to deserve this? I'm just a poor black girl, in the messed up evil —"

I was in the middle of speaking, and I was interrupted with a hand clap. It was Mr. Knox, and he was making his way towards me.

"Come on. That's enough," he said as he grabbed my hair.

"I didn't do anything. Please don't take me back to the hell hole."

"I had to stop you because you seemed as if you were going to add me in your Godly poem."

"No, sir, I wasn't going to ever mention you to anyone. What we did here will stay here. I understand you and your ways. I know why you're the way you are. This world really revolves around your kind, and us blacks are just living here with your permission."

"You mean you niggers!" he said as I got a whiff of his breath.

"Yes, master. You know that's what I meant."

"That's more like it," he said as he told me to have a seat. "We have to go over your release papers. This one states that you will report to the probation office at nine A.M. sharp. You cannot do drugs, or you will be in violation of the terms of your parole, and you will come back in here with me. All I need is for you to get to that safe, so, if you come back in here, I will kill you myself. I killed a nigger bitch before, and I will kill again. Is that understood? Do I make myself clear?" he said as he handed me a pen to sign on the dotted line.

"Sure, master. I will do what I am told. Can I please finish my poem?" I asked as I signed my name.

"You have about five minutes."

I walked back in, and the girls were looking at me like they wanted me to finish. "The floor is yours," Ms. Allgood said.

I stood in front of them and spoke.

There is a GOD. I just want all of you girls to know.
All of the work that He does will not always show.
Just because we can't see him, don't think that he's not here.
He has always been with us. He has always been near.
He's done so much for us as the whole world could see
And he placed us all exactly where he wanted us to be

I wanted to leave them with peace of mind and assure them that there was a God. I wanted them to know that He was with them when they were asleep. He was with them when they were doing bad. He was even with them when they had committed their crimes. The warden had made a different bible. I remember the first time I looked in it. They had changed scriptures, and they didn't even have Revelations in their bible. I was going to take all of them down when the time was right.

"Everyone, give Tasha Jean a round of applause. Hopefully, she won't make her way back like some of you do. It's time to go get on the bus," Mr. Knox said as he led the way. "I have all of your information, and I will have eyes watching you like a hawk. You better stick to the plan, so I can get the fuck out of this place."

I headed for the bus. As I was getting on the bus, I felt so sorry for the girls that were getting off. Some of them had smiles on their faces. They just didn't know what they were about to get into. I sat on a seat by the window. I was the only one on the bus. The bus driver kept watching me through the rear view mirror, but he had spoken to me when I stepped on, and I felt a good vibe from him. He was probably a black man just doing his job. When we pulled off, we were surrounded by woods and trees. I couldn't find my way back there even if I had a map. There were too many trees and so many turns. I sat by the window and watched the livestock as we hit the road. I enjoyed watching the calves with their mothers. Then, I started to get sad because that reminded me of Mama. She had crazy ways, but, if she were alive, at least, I could see her again. The fact that her murder was unsolved didn't make any sense to me. Who would want to kill my mama? Everyone in my neighborhood had nice homes and fast cars. We even had a nice house. Mama didn't work, but she kept the utilities on, and she kept a spotless house. It still puzzled me how she paid our bills because all she did was drink beer and smoke cigarettes. The ride even seemed longer going back to freedom. I laid my head on the window and fell asleep.

21
Home Sweet Home

"We're here, ma'am," the driver said as we pulled up at a Greyhound station.

"How am I supposed to get home from here? I live on a rocky road in the country. That place can't get anything right. If anything, they're screwing the poor girls up. They don't rehabilitate; they masturbate. All of them are sick in there, and I'm going to deal with them as soon as I find out who murdered my mama."

"Did they give you an envelope?"

"Yes."

"May I see it please?"

I handed him the envelope, and there was a voucher in there for fifty dollars for cab fare.

"All you have to do is go get in one of them cabs and sign this here voucher over to them. Good luck."

"Thank you so much," I said as I got off.

I went to a cab and gave him mama's address. I really didn't want to live in our house anymore. As we entered my neighborhood and rode down the rocky road, the first house that I saw was the Kennedy's house. It had a FOR SALE sign in the yard. The first thing that came across my mind was that they had found Spyder's cash and hauled ass. When I got to the Johnson's house, there was something different about it, too. They had burglar bars all around it. Then, I thought maybe the Kennedys had moved because they thought that the killer would strike again. It had been a year, and I hadn't heard anything. I couldn't hear anything being locked away in that maximum YDC facility.

"Those bastards didn't even mail my letters to J.J."

One day, I had watched Mr. Knox set my letters fire. Then, he pissed on them, putting them out.

"Right here is fine," I said as the driver slammed on the brakes in front of J.J's house. I didn't want to look over at my house, but I couldn't help it, so I took a quick glance over there, and I saw a car in the yard. Who could that be? I wondered if that was the probation officer. *I haven't been out a full twenty-four hours, and they were fucking with me already,* I thought as I rang Ms. Johnson's doorbell.

"Who is it?" she sounded like she was unlocking a time machine. She must have had at least ten deadbolts on that door from the top to the bottom.

"It's me. Tasha Jean," I said, looking past her to see if I could see J.J.

She had a surprised look on her face when she opened up the door and saw that it was me.

"Did you break out of jail?"

"No, don't be silly. I got out on good behavior. Where's J.J?" I asked as I looked around.

"He's not here. He will be going off to college soon. He's going to Harvard to become a doctor."

"When will he be back? I would love to see him before he leaves."

"I don't know. Ever since he graduated, he has been partying. I am starting to see traits of his father in him."

There was something different about her. She talked to me so coldly and dryly. When I would ask her a question about J.J., she wouldn't look me in my face. She didn't even hug me when I walked in. *Maybe, her husband did leave her for a black woman.* Maybe, Spyder was right. I got the feeling that she had wanted me to stay locked up until J.J. went away to college, but I had thirty million reasons why he should skip Harvard. He could start the rock band he wanted so badly, and we could get out of this place. I was about to ask her another question about J.J., but she cut me off and walked to the window.

"That car has been parked over there all week," she said as she opened up the curtain, looking at Mama's house. "There is a lady living over there."

"Well, did you ask her who she was? Is she like a live-in probation lady or something?"

"I didn't ask her, but I noticed that she's started a nice vegetable garden in the back."

"Well, was it Mama?"

I don't know why I asked that question since Mama was deader than a doornail.

"Can you please tell J.J. to come by when he gets back?"

"Sure," she said as she opened the door.

I looked in the window first to see who was in Mama's house. The window was up, and the curtains were pulled up.

"Come on in here," I heard a familiar woman's voice say.

From a distance, she looked like a ghost because, the closer I got, the more she looked just like Mama.

"What's the matter? You don't know your own family when you see her?"

"Who are you?" I nervously asked. I thought I was staring Mama in the face.

"Child, don't be silly. I'm your grandmother. Your mother used to have a picture of me on her wall. I used to be right over there next to Dr. King's picture, which is missing by the way."

As I looked around the house, I noticed that it had been redecorated.

"Excuse me, but what is your name?"

"My name is Grandma," she said as she walked over and hugged me. "Child, you are shaking like a leaf." She held me tight. "What's the matter? You look like you've just seen a ghost?"

"You look exactly like my mama," I said as I stood back and looked her up and down. She even had the same beer breath as Mama.

"Well, I'm not your mama; I'm your grandma. And never mind my name. You can just call me Grandma."

"Lady, you expect me to believe that bullshit-ass story? That you're my fucking grandma? My mama didn't talk about her mother much, but I know, for a fact, that her mother is dead! I don't know who you are, but I am not staying here with you," I said as I ran for the door.

"You will sit your ass down, or I will call that nice Mr. Knox and have your ass hauled back to juvenile."

"How do you know him?" I asked suspiciously.

"I told you. I am your grandma. I know a lot of shit." She had a wicked look on her face.

22
Granny's Rules

I went into my room and looked for some clues, hoping that the killer had left something behind, but the house was smelling like the power of Pine Sol. I didn't know what I was looking for, but I was going to start off by sneaking in Mama's room. It was Granny's room now.

I thought that it was strange that she didn't have any tears in her eyes when she spoke of my mother. Who was this lady? She didn't say anything about a funeral. She didn't say anything at all, pertaining to her murdered daughter. They were identical, though. They both were short, light skinned with a short curly afro.

I wanted to soak in a tub of hot water, but I was too scared to close my eyes in with this stranger in the house. I was going to find out who she was one way or another.

I walked to the edge of the hallway and peeped in on my so-called grandma. She didn't even look like a grandma. She did not have one strand of gray hair. She was standing there, looking at the wall like she was having a conversation with it, but I noticed that she was talking to someone at the back door. She was as nutty as a fruitcake if she thought I believed that she was my grandma. She closed the back door and said, "Tasha Jean, come on in here. It's time that I break the rules down to you."

I had a hard time looking at this lady's face, knowing that Mama was dead, and she looked identical to her. Identical? That's it. Mama could have had a twin sister, but Mama never talked about anyone but her mother. *Maybe, she is my grandma*, I thought as I looked at her.

"Can I call you Mama since you look so much like her?"

"No! You will call me Grandma! Now, listen up. I will see to it that you report to the probation office every week. You will look for a job."

" A job? But I'm only sixteen! Can I go back to school?"

"The GED that you got in that place should be equivalent."

She had a smart mouth, and I didn't like that about her. She was a funny acting grandma.

"My mother's name is Lynn. What's yours?" I said, trying to change the subject.

"Your mama's name is Lynette, and I'm Annette, and we like to ride in corvettes," she said like she was about to cheer. "I mean my name is Bertha. Child, just call me Grandma B. Now, where was I?" She looked around. She was on something because she was jittery and very anxious. "I have a garden back there, and it's your job to water it every day. As you can see, I am in tip top shape, so that means we will go jogging every morning."

"I know that you get up in the wee hours to exercise. My mother was in tip top shape as well."

"Well, you see where she gets it from then."

I kept bringing up Mama and, for a woman who had lost her daughter, she seemed to be very happy go lucky. One thing she and Mama had in common, they wouldn't let me get a word in. Her mouth had been on talk mode ever since I walked in the house.

"I think I covered everything. Do you have any questions?"

I wanted to say, "Yes, I have a question. Who the fuck are you?"

"Oh, one more thing. If you smoke weed, you have to bring me some, too."

"I can't smoke. I am on probation, remember?"

"Child, we'll go into town and get some cleaner to clean your system out."

I was really suspicious of her now.

"If you get some of that good weed, give your granny just a little hit."

I really wished that she would stop calling herself granny because she could go for my sister. I wanted to test her and see where her head was at.

"Aren't you scared to live here after someone killed your daughter in this very same living room that we are standing in now?"

"I'm not scared of the dead. If anything, you should be more afraid of the living," she said with one eyebrow raised. "Besides, I have a gun under your mama's bed. I will blow a motherfucker's head off."

"About that. How could you sleep in her bed?"

"She has twelve hundred tread count sheets. I sleep like I an angel on a soft cloud."

I looked at her legs, and she looked like she could have been a track star. There was a knock at the door, and she motioned for me to be still. She went in Mama's room and retrieved a .357 revolver from under the bed.

"Who is it?" she asked as she went to the door with the gun in her hand.

"This is J.J. from next door."

"Who are you looking for?"

"It's J.J.," I said as I reached for the door knob.

"She can't have no company," she said as she snatched my hand off of the door knob.

"I have something very important to tell her."

"J.J., call me on the house phone," I screamed at the door.

"The house phone is off," she said with a grin on her face.

"Lady, Granny, whoever you is, you better open that door and let me see him."

"I am a bitch with a gun. How dare you talk to me like that?"

I took a deep breath, turned around, and went to my room. I knew, for a fact, that she wasn't my grandma, but who could she be? Was she Mama, and mama really wasn't dead? I didn't know what to think, but I knew that that granny bitch had to go.

23
Sweet Dreams

"Push harder," the doctor said as I pushed with all my might.

"I can't it hurts so bad!"

"Come on. This is no different from the last two times."

"Push, baby! I can see his head."

J.J. was dressed in doctor's attire. He held my hand and said, "Tasha Jean, just give it one big hard push. You're doing great."

I felt the baby's head come out. My pussy felt like it was ripping apart. I heard a loud cry, and my baby had been born.

"It's a boy!" the doctor said as he held my baby upside down. As I stood up, I saw Mama and Ms. Johnson. They were both overjoyed. They were both in tears, but I should have been the one crying. I was the one in excruciating pain.

"How are you feeling, sweetheart?" Mama asked.

"I feel like my whole pussy is on fire," I said as I reached for her hand.

"That's called natural childbirth. I felt the same way when I had you, but it will all be over soon, as soon as the meds kick in."

"Thanks for being here, Mama. This means so much to me."

"You know I wouldn't miss this day for nothing in the world," she said as she watched the doctor weigh the baby. "I am so proud of you. You've married the love of your life. I love the Victorian home that you guys live in."

"I am proud to say that you have given birth to a nine pound baby boy," the doctor said as he handed my baby to one of the nurses. J.J. and Ms. Johnson were on one side, and Mama was on the other side.

"I am so glad that you're my daughter-in-law," Ms. Johnson said. "I just want to know one thing. How many kids do y'all plan on having? This is the fourth child you have had in six years. J.J. Jr. already has enough playmates. The twins Justin and Zack are a handful."

"Well, one more won't hurt. Besides, J.J. and I want to have a big family," I smiled.

J.J brought my little bundle of joy to me. He was sleeping peacefully.

"We're going to name him Jeremy," I said as I kissed my precious bundle of joy.

"You can't seem to have a girl to save your life," Mama joked. "I am the proud grandma of four cute, smart, handsome boys. I will come by your house and fix you a hot meal later."

"That's not necessary," J.J. said. "Our servants have everything covered."

"Well, excuse me, Mr. Rock Star," Mama said.

" J.J., Mama can come over and cook for me if she wants to."

Mama held the baby and told me that she would come visit me when I arrived home from the hospital.

The next day, we pulled up to our home in our Cadillac CTS sports wagon. When we arrived at our home, the boys flew out the house to greet us. They couldn't wait to see the new addition to our family. J.J. Jr. was eight, the twins Justin and Zack were five, and baby Jeremy was only a few days old. I was so happy that J.J and I had finally tied the knot.

"Tasha Jean, wake up! Tasha Jean, wake up!"

I turned around and stretched my arms to the ceiling, and this crazy lady was in my face, blowing a whistle, looking just like Mama.

"I know you're used to these whistles," she said as

she pulled my covers back. "It's time to go jogging."

She was standing there in exercise attire. She even had a sweatband around her head. I was having the best dream in my life, and she had to come and stop it all.

"Can I shower first?"

"No need to shower before you exercise. What sense does that make?" she said as she jogged in place.

"Well, can I, at least, brush my teeth?" I said as I rolled my eyes and headed for the bathroom.

"I will be downstairs waiting," she said as she headed to go downstairs.

When I got back in my room, I noticed that there was something different. My YDC uniform wasn't on the floor where I had left it. *Now, she has crossed the line.* I put on some sweats and a shirt and headed downstairs. When I got downstairs, she was stretching in front of the television.

"Come and join me," she said as she did a windmill. "We don't want to cramp up out there. Besides, what if we have to run for our lives? What if a dog gets behind us? We have to be able to outrun a dog," she said as she power walked back and forth.

"Whatever," I said as I joined her and stretched. She began to count out loud.

"That's enough," she said as she grabbed the keys to lock up the house.

When we got outside, the sound of the birds chirping was music to my ears. She started jogging quickly, and I lagged behind. I glanced back at her garden, and it was made in a trail that led to the back of the Kennedy's house. I looked at J.J.'s house. No cars were in the yard. As we jogged quietly, I looked up at the Kennedy's house, and it looked deserted. As I jogged, I thought about the dream that I was having before I was rudely interrupted by the crazy lady. I had four boys with J.J. I really hoped that that dream came true. I wondered what he was thinking when Miss Psycho told him that I couldn't have company. I wondered what did he have to tell me? All sorts of questions were going through my head, and, before I knew it, we were back at the house.

"Go on up there and shower. It's time for you to go report," I heard the crazy lady say.

"Where did you put my YDC uniform?"

I had just remembered the envelope that I'd found in Mr. Knox's hell hole. I'd put it up in the attic.

"I know you don't want to be reminded of that place."

Getting up at six in the morning is being reminded of that place, I thought. After I got dressed, I went to the kitchen to fix a bowl of cereal. I looked in on her in the living room, and she was drinking a beer and smoking a cigarette just like Mama used to do. *She didn't cook either,* I thought as I shoved a spoon full of Pops in my mouth.

24
(Some) Black People Shouldn't be in Charge

The crazy lady and I got in her four door black sedan and headed downtown to the probation office. She turned the radio up loud when Aretha Franklin's "Chain of Fools" came on. As I listened to the words, Aretha said that she was just a link in his chain. She said that she was in a chain of fools. I wanted to be a link in J.J.'s chain. I wouldn't care if I was the rusted part.

She drove fast, like a bat out of hell. She wasn't following the speed limits at all. We finally pulled up at a tall, red building.

"I'll stay in the car," she said as she put the car in park.

I walked in, and I signed my name and waited. I glanced at the strict rules that were to be obeyed by ALL probationers. They read as follows: *No talking. No cell phones. No asking secretary, "How long do I have to wait?" No sleeping. No in and out. No hats. No tank tops. No shades. No restrooms. Drug tests are mandatory. At that time, all probationers get to use the restroom.*

"Tasha Jean Jones! Tasha Jeans Jones!" I heard the receptionist call my name, but she didn't give me time to answer.

"Here," I said as I stood up.

"Walk up to this window," she said as she sat a clipboard outside of the window. "You didn't check the amount you're paying today."

"What amount? I have to pay?"

"Yes. Your fine is five thousand dollars."

"Five thousand dollars!"

"Ma'am, this is my first time here, and I don't know anything about a fine."

"My name is Ms. Nelson," she said as she pointed at her name tag.

"Well, Ms. Nelson, I just got out yesterday, and no one told me I had to have money. I was only told that I had to report to this place for five years."

"Have a seat until your probation officer calls you," she said as she slammed the window shut.

I looked around and saw that everyone in there was sitting up straight, looking in one direction. They were facing the wall ahead.

"What the fuck is wrong with her?" I said as I looked at the other probationers.

No one said anything. I took a seat and laid back in the chair. I was tired from all that jogging so early in the morning.

"Get up!" I heard a man's voice say. "Young lady, get up! There is no sleeping in here! Can't you read?" He pointed at the rules. "Rule number four — no sleeping! Look around. Do you see how everyone else is positioned in their seats?"

"Yeah."

"It's not 'yeah'; it's 'yes, sir', and, if you want to do things your way, I could see to it that you go back to prison."

"I wasn't in prison," I snapped.

"You will be if I make you do your five years that you have on paper. Stand in the corner until your probation officer calls you," he said as he left and slammed the door.

I turned around and looked at the other probationers. They were still looking like zombies. *All this judicial system shit is just the same*, I thought as I turned around and faced the wall. *They act like we owe them something. If they're not happy with their jobs, they should choose something else.* I stood there for about an hour, listening to everyone's name being called except mine. I was tired of standing up, so I sat down in the corner.

"You don't hear too well, do you?" the black man said, screaming in my ear.

"I've been standing up for hours. When are y'all going to call me back there?"

"You just violated your probation, and I got the mind to send you back to the slammer!"

I felt all eyes on me because he stood me there and roasted me like a drill sergeant. The receptionist tapped on the window to get his attention. He looked at me and said, "I'm not done with you."

I looked as he walked over to her, and she showed him my file. He walked back over and kindly said, "Tasha Jean Jones, please follow me."

I don't know what she showed him, but he quickly changed his tone with me.

"Stand right here against the wall and spread your legs."

"Am I being arrested again?"

"An officer will be in here to search you before you go back to see your probation officer."

I stood there with my hands on the wall and my legs spread as far as I could. After about five minutes, a short black female officer came in. She had on a black collar shirt, khaki cargo pants, and a pair of black, shiny, hi tech boots. She had her hair pulled back in a ponytail with a pair of Kenneth Cole specks on.

"I'm Officer Brady, and I will be searching you to make sure you don't have any weapons on you. Then, I will take you to the back to have a drug screening."

"Weapons," I said as I smirked.

"Do you find something funny?" she said as she began to pat me down.

"No, you used the word weapons like I am a terrorist or something."

"Before we begin this search, I will ask you. Are there any weapons in your pocket?"

"No," I said with a grin on my face.

She turned me around by the back of my neck and slammed me against the wall.

"Did I say something funny?" she said with her forearm at my throat.

I was gasping for air, I couldn't speak and all I could do was shake my head.

"Do you see something funny now?" she asked as she put more pressure on her forearm. Again, I shook my head.

"Go on. Laugh now," she said as I smelled the loud onion smell on her breath. "Go ahead and make my day. You were just grinning and smirking a few seconds ago. Now, you've bit off more than you can chew."

She released her arm. I was breathing hard, trying to catch my breath. I felt myself about to tear up, but I thought back to my treatment at YDC, so I straightened up my clothes, looked her in her eyes, and said, "Officer Brady, there are no weapons in my pocket."

"Good," she said as she told me to assume the position again. As I turned back around, I saw the man who was screaming at me earlier at the door, watching her pat me down.

"She's good," she said as she looked in his direction. He pointed at me and told me to follow him. We walked down the hall to my probation officer's office. I walked in and had a seat. She was on the phone, so I looked around. I observed her pictures and rewards on the wall. She even had a picture with the president! She must be the best probation officer in the world to take a picture with the President of the United States. When I saw the picture of her with the president, I wondered if I could confide in her about the treatment at the YDC facility. I looked around to see if I could spot any pictures of her family, but I didn't see any, which led me to believe that she was all about her work. When she hung up the phone, she didn't say anything. She looked through my file. She didn't look mean like the others, but what did mean look like? The receptionist looked like a nerd, but she shouted at me when I signed in. I sat up straight in the chair. I didn't slouch. The more I looked at that picture of the president, the more I wanted to tell her about DON'T GET THEM RIGHT CORRECTIONAL FACILITY. She got up and walked in front of me and leaned on her desk and said, "I'm Mrs. Reynolds. I will be supervising you for the next five years."

I looked at her name tag on her desk and noticed that she was married. *Good,* I thought. *At least, she is getting dick in her life.* Her nails were freshly manicured. Her hair was in curls all the way to the middle of her back, and she was dressed differently from the others. She had on a two piece skirt set.

"Yes, ma'am," I said as I looked at another one of her awards that read *Top Fugitive Parole Agent.* I was relieved to know that she was highly trained. Her spirit to me seemed like she was a person that I could trust.

"We can get through these five years smooth as butter. It all depends on you," she said as she closed the door. "This is your job search paper. You have to get this signed by each employer, so I know that you have been seeking employment."

I looked at the paper, and there were fifty slots on there.

"You have to look for fifty jobs per month. You have to report to me once a week, so I can see that you've been looking. Once you find employment, you will report to me once a month. And I will drop by whenever I feel like it, to make sure you're not disrespecting your grandma. By the way, I am so sorry about what happened to your mother."

When she said that, I felt my heart skip a beat. I wanted to show her the notebook that I had stolen from Mr. Knox's hell hole. When she showed me sympathy, I knew right then and there that I could confide in her. She made me feel real good. She hadn't raised her voice at me. She actually talked to me like I was a human being. When she gave me my appointment card for the following week, I wanted to hug her because no one had ever been that nice to me. She told me to go down the hall and make a left and take a drug screen. There was a short line, and I stood in it for only a moment before it was my turn. The same officer that had searched me was the one doing the drug screens. *This is going to be fun*, I thought as I thumped my appointment card. The men were on one side, and the women were on the other side. She told me to grab a cup and bring it to her. She wrote my name on it and told me to follow her. When we got to the bathroom, she stood at the door while I went in. There was no sign of her leaving, so I pulled my pants down and pissed in the cup. I didn't bother asking her anything because I didn't want her to put me in another choke hold. She watched me until the last drip dropped. I handed her the cup, and she pointed for me to put it in the slot on the wall.

When I walked out and got in the car, the crazy lady

was blasting the music, listening to the O'jays' "Stairway To Heaven". I didn't say anything. I just let the seat back and listened to Eddie Levert sing his lungs out.

She didn't have no respect for the speed limits once again. I wished a policeman would have pulled her over and locked her up. Maybe then, I could have found out her real identity.

25
Looking for a Job

I had been eating cereal and Hamburger Helper since I'd gotten out. Maybe, she was my relative because Mama didn't cook either. Every morning, she did the same things that Mama used to do. She smoked cigarettes, drank beer, and watched soap operas. She didn't have men over, but I've often heard her masturbating at night.

I woke up and walked downstairs to ask her if she was going to take me to look for a job. She told me that I had to walk. I put on a pair of cut up jeans and a t-shirt. I grabbed my job search paper and walked out the door.

"You be back before dark, you hear?"

I walked past J.J's house and saw Jessica's car there. I didn't want to face them together. *Maybe, he felt sorry for me when I got in trouble. Maybe, he told me that he would marry me to help me keep my sanity while I was locked up.* I didn't have anywhere to go look for work. The only store around was Old Man Charles' Corner Store, and it was family owned. As I got to the end of the street, I looked up at the Kennedy's house and wondered where they'd moved to. I walked to the corner store and found Old Man Charles sitting on a stool, watching *Sanford and Son*.

"Can you sign this paper for me please?" I asked as I walked in.

He looked at me and said, "I thought you had to do some time."

"I did, but I got out on good behavior."

"Is that right?" he said as he grabbed his glasses and

looked at the paper.

"You don't have to hire me. You can just sign it so that my probation officer knows that I have, in fact, been looking for a job."

"You have to go to the new shopping center," he said as he signed the paper.

"What new shopping center?"

"There is one about a mile down the road."

"A mile down?" I asked.

"Yes, just follow the dirt road to the end, and you will see all those buildings that the crackers done built. Can you believe they had to nerve to try and buy me out? This store was started by my great-granddaddy, and I will not sell to them or anyone else. Oh, and another thing, I am sorry about Lynnette. She was a really sweet lady, but I could have sworn I saw someone who looked just like her come in the other day and get a twelve pack of beer and cigarettes, just like she used to. She looked identical to your mother, but I'm just an old man and my sight isn't too good these days, so I could be wrong."

He was right, but I didn't want to get into any details about the crazy lady because I didn't even know who she really was. He called my mama Lynette, and I only knew her as Lynn. That was a shame that I didn't know my own mother's name. I had heard her name from somewhere before, and it was from Mr. Knox. He had mentioned that he used to date a nigger bitch named Lynette. My heart skipped several beats before it went back to its regular rhythm.

I thought about walking to the new shopping center, but I changed my mind. I wanted to go home and read that notebook that I got from the YDC. I walked home slowly kicking the rocks on the dirt road. I looked at Spyder's house. I wanted to break in and go get the money out of the safe, but where would I put it. Plus, Mr. Knox told me not to make a move until he contacted me. I walked past J.J.'s house and Jessica's silver BMW was still in the yard. I walked in the house, and the crazy lady wasn't on the sofa watching TV. I walked in on her, and she was on the telephone. She had told me that the home phone was off. I tip toed and listened as she said: "So far, the plan is going good. She's falling for it. I even made a garden so that she thinks I am a granny for real. I told you that I should have put on a gray wig because she is a little suspicious about my hair. I feel so bad for treating her so badly. I want to tell her so bad, but I trust you and I know that you will catch that son of a bitch. I owe it to my sister. She was trying to help me out, and I got her killed. She was my twin, and I thought of this plan to catch that bastard in the act. I got to go. I think she just walked in," she said as she hung up the phone.

When she walked in, I acted like I had just walked in.

"Hey, Grandma B! I had fun job hunting," I said as I ran upstairs.

I knew all of my answers were in Mama's room. I sat on my bed and looked at the picture I had of Mama on my nightstand. I picked it up and said, "Mama, please send me a sign. Mama, please help me. There is a lady here, and she wants me to believe that she's your mother, but I know better. Did you have a twin sister that I didn't know about? Mama, I know you're here in spirit, and I know we weren't the best of friends. But I need you and God to help me figure this one out."

I kissed the picture as I placed it back on the night stand. I remembered where the notebook was, and I opened it up and began to read. The first page was from a girl name Susan.

I only have five more days here, but Ms. Allgood told me that she could make that turn
into another year.
I did everything that she told me to do.
I even dyed my hair blue.
She said it wasn't about the respect; it was about the power,
And she made my life miserable by the hour.
She did things with me like jump in the shower,
And she enjoyed playing in my pussy for hours.
She had so many girls in check.
Some of them even left here in a nervous wreck.
These people in here are the true definitions of evil.
They had done so much bad to the good people.
I wanted to get out and tell on them all,
But I didn't know who in the world I could call.
I told another one of the girls my plan,
And Ms. Allgood beat me like a man.
She turned my five days into another year.
I took my own life by piercing my brain through my ear.

"Rest in peace, Susan," I said as I read more.
The next page was from a girl named Pudding.
If I don't get out of this place soon,
I am going to kill myself with a spoon.
The way they treat us isn't fair.
All I needed was my parents just to be there
I didn't even do the crime,
But I was found guilty and had to do some time.
I was at the wrong place,
And I ended up with a gun in my face.
We were just going to buy some weed,
And we were their victims in their time of need.
We got robbed at the dope house

And Spanky came back like mighty mouse.
He shot that whole house up
And I was the driver of his truck.
We got stopped shortly after.
When we saw blue lights, I heard laughter.
I was just hanging with my peers.
I didn't know driving a truck could get you seven years.

"Damn, Pudding! You was at the wrong place at the wrong time, and you wasn't just driving a truck— you were an accessory to a crime."
The next page was written by a girl named Phyllis.
Something has to be done about this place.
They keep invading my space.
I mailed several letters to my folks,
But they take mail here for a joke.
The warden is the worst of them all.
She cut off my pinky because I laughed when she was about to fall.
I have something bigger,
And it shoots six times with a trigger.
Now, hold your hand straight,
And your blood better not get on my face.
She chopped it off real smooth,
And I was walking around looking like a fool.
I never knew that I could feel so much pain
She said that she should have cut my main vein.

I closed the notebook, I was going to tell on them. I had to mail this notebook to the president, but I didn't have the address. I wanted to tell somebody because no one deserved to be treated the way we were treated.

26
Probation

That notebook I had was more than enough information to put them all away. They all needed to be locked up and tortured like they had done to us. Mr. Knox, Ms. Allgood, and the warden needed to be taught a lesson. I was going to bring them down.

The same thing had been going on for weeks. She was plugging up the phone and using it only when she needed. And I was pretending that she was my grandma. I walked downstairs, and I told her that I was ready to go report. She didn't even wake me up to go jogging anymore. We hopped in her black sedan, and she did the same thing— blast the music and speed like she was in a NASCAR race.

We pulled up to the red building, and, once again, she stayed in the car while I went to report. I signed in and sat down like the others. No one said anything to one another. I made sure I put zero by the amount that I was paying today. I didn't have a job, and I couldn't give them what I didn't have. Mrs. Reynolds called me, and I followed her to her office. I handed her my job search paper, and she looked at it and said, "Is this a joke?"

Old Man Charles signature was on there fifty times.

"No, this isn't a joke. I live in the country, and we only have one corner store and it is family-owned."

She looked up my address and told me that there was a new shopping center that I could go to.

"I know. Old Man Charles mentioned that to me, but I don't have a car. And the crazy lady that I live with won't take me anywhere."

"What do you mean 'the crazy lady that you live with'? You have to have a responsible adult to help you out. You're only seventeen for crying out loud. We will have to place you in foster care if your guardian doesn't take full responsibility."

"I would love to go to foster care," I said, looking her dead in her eyes. I couldn't help it anymore. I broke down and told her everything that was going on. I wasn't a fool. I wasn't going to tell her about the thirty million. "Better yet. I have a notebook that would close that YDC down for good."

"What are you talking about?" she asked as she got up and closed the door.

"Please tell me that I can trust you first because I could get killed for the stuff I'm about to tell you."

"Scouts honor," she said as she put her hand over her heart. "A dear old friend of mine is running that place. His name is Special Agent Utah. He's really a great guy."

"I was put in jail for nothing. I was charged with two kilos of cocaine that was initially five, but the old timer took two."

Then, something clicked in my head when she said Special Agent Utah. He was the dirty old timer that came to me in the hospital. Could Special Agent Utah and Mr. Knox be the same person? I didn't know whether I should confide in her since she was a good friend of Mr. Knox's. He had to be Special Agent Utah because he was the only man there running shit. I didn't know how much she knew, so I decided to only tell her a little bit. I sat back in the chair, and my tongue started moving.

"That man that you call a good friend called me a nigger bitch seven days a week, twenty four hours a day. That man that you call a good friend raped me repeatedly in there. That good friend of yours made me call him master while I was sucking his dick. That good friend—"

"I get it," she said as she interrupted me. "Look at me." She handed me Kleenex to wipe my tears. "I will look into this. You have my word. In the meantime, here is a bus pass, so you can go to that shopping center and look for a job." She gave me my next appointment card and told me not to worry about the drug screen.

27
Job Hunting

"Going job hunting!" I screamed to the crazy lady as I walked out the door. I turned around, and she was looking at me out the window in Mama's room. She reminded me of how Mama used to look at me after she put me out. I walked past J.J.'s house and Jessica's car wasn't there, but there was a pink tricycle in the yard. Maybe, one of his little cousins were over. I wanted to go knock on the door, but I was too scared. I'd seen Jessica's car over there damn near every day. Maybe, they were going steady. I didn't ride the bus. I decided to walk to the shopping center. It was only a mile. I had walked more than that at the YDC. When I got to the end of the street, I saw an unmarked police car. I knew what I wasn't going to do and that was get in the car with anyone ever again. I saw a tall white man get out, and, as I got closer, I noticed that it was Mr. Knox. I almost shit my pants because my first thought was that he was going to kill me because I had reported him. I had my hands in my pockets. I wanted to take off running, but I knew he would catch me and kill me.

"Are you ready to get this plan in motion?" he said as he spit black stuff on the ground.

"Yes, master," I said gladly because he didn't know what Mrs. Reynolds and I had talked about yet.

"Now, this is the deal. That house is going to be sold in the next few months. You have to go in there and get the money out of the safe."

I wanted to ask him why he couldn't do it himself because no one would see him. The Kennedy's house sat on a hill, and Spyder's house sat directly behind it. He handed me a bag of tools and told me how to pick the lock. Now that I think back, he was the dirty old timer who Spyder was talking about. I remembered him from the hospital. I could never forget those rotten teeth.

"Open the bag."

I opened the bag, and he had a hammer in there along with a screwdriver and some pliers.

"This looks like it will get the job done, master."

"I will meet you here at this same time next month. You can cut that master shit out. Focus on my money in the safe," he said as he jumped in the car and sped off.

I wanted to be in a courtroom testifying against his ass at this same time next month. I power walked all the way to the new shopping center. The streets still smelled like freshly paved tar. There were so many different places to choose from. I decided to walk in all of the fast foods first. Then, I decided to try the clothing stores. The first fast food place I walked in was Taco Bell.

"Welcome to Taco Bell! How can I help you?"

"Are you guys hiring?"

"Are we what?" the cashier she said as she scratched her tired ass wig.

"Can I speak with a manager?"

"The manager ain't here, and you ain't gone take my job either."

"I don't want your job."

I didn't bother getting my paper signed. After going to all of the fast food restaurants, I went to a clothing store. The manager was at the register.

"Are you guys hiring?" I politely asked.

He grabbed an application and told me to fill it out right now. I filled it out and handed it back to him. He looked over it and said, "You left this one blank."

It was the one asking me if I was a convicted felon. I was, but I needed a job, and I didn't want to explain my background to him. I grabbed the paper and checked the yes box.

"I admire your honesty."

I just knew he was going to kick me out of his store.

"I don't want to know what you did. We have cameras all over this place, so if you snooze, you lose."

"You won't be sorry, Mr. Stokes."

"I believe in giving young people a chance. Plus, you all are the future," he said. Mr. Stokes was a middle aged black man. And he had on a gold wedding band. There were some good people still left in the world, and he was the second nice person that I'd met.

"Be here at nine A.M. sharp. Melisa, the assistant manager, will train you."

I was so happy. I skipped all the way home. When I got home, J.J. was sitting on his porch.

"Come here," he said as I walked by. I stood there for a moment and decided to go.

"I missed you, and I've been trying to see you so many times. Who is that crazy lady that is over there? She looks just like Lynn."

"I know she does, but I don't know who she is. She claims that she's my grandma, but she's dead. I think she's Mama's evil twin."

"That is weird," he said as he grabbed my hand. "So, how have you been?"

"I've been making it," I said as I watched Ms. Johnson come outside with a pretty baby girl.

"She's awake," she said as she handed the baby to J.J.

"Is this your niece?" I asked as I rubbed her head.

"No, this is his daughter and don't rub the top of her head. Her soft spot is up there."

"Thanks, Mother! I was going to tell her."

That explained the tricycle in their front yard. I was hurt that J.J had a baby by that slut Jessica.

"What's her name?" I said as I wiped the slobber out of her mouth.

"You mean you're not mad?"

"J.J., of course not. I have so much on my plate right now that I don't have time for anything else. I am trying to find myself. I want to find my daddy and live with him for the rest of my life."

"Her name is Chelsea, and she is nine months old. Are you sure she is yours because she don't look like you?"

"Jessica has told me that I'm the only boy that she was sleeping with. Plus, my mom says she has my feet."

That baby didn't look shit like J.J. That baby had a head like Stewie from *Family Guy*.

28
First Day on the Job

I woke up bright and early to get ready for work. I was so ready to train for my new job. The crazy lady was doing the same shit, drinking beers and watching TV. I put on my uniform and walked out the door. I was proud to walk with a uniform that didn't have numbers on it. I looked next door and I saw J.J., Jessica, and the baby. They looked like one big, happy family, but I saw J.J. watching me with my peripheral vision.

"Go to Daddy," Jessica said loudly enough for me to hear.

I walked to work, and I was the first one there. The other employees began to show up one by one.

"You must be Tasha Jean," the assistant manager said as she unlocked the door.

I don't know why I thought that the assistant manager would be old, but Melisa was a young, white girl. She gave me a tour of the store, and she also told me that we had a twenty percent discount that we could use for ourselves and family.

"Which reminds me. My brother Chad and his fiancée will be here any minute to use mine," she said as she looked at her watch.

She kept talking about her brother and his new baby. She said that her parents thought that she was going to get a baby first. While we were at the register, Jessica and another dude and her baby walked in.

"Hey, sister-in-law," Melisa said as she grabbed Jessica's baby.

When Jessica saw me, her face damn near cracked.

"Chad, go pick out the clothes for the baby, and the new cashier can ring you up, using my discount. Jess, what's up? You look like you just seen a ghost," Melisa said.

She did, I thought, *and that ghost is me.* I knew that wasn't J.J's baby. That baby didn't look anything like him. Chad came back with a buggy full of clothes. He had everything from Keds to Osh Gosh B Gosh piled up in the buggy.

"Your niece is lovely, Melisa," I said as I looked at Jessica.

"Jess carried her, but I did all the work," Chad said. "I even named her."

Jessica just stood there speechless. She was busted, and I was going to tell the love of my life. J.J. had to know the truth. He was a great guy. After I rung them up, Melisa helped Chad take the bags to the car. It was just me and Jessica left at the register. She looked at me and said, "You will not!"

"Want to bet?"

"Wait!" she said as she slung her hair out of her face. I actually got a closer look at her, and she had freckles all in her face. What the hell did J.J see in her?

"What do you want from me?"

"I want you to stay the hell away from my man. I am in love with him. I have been in love with him since the fifth grade."

"I will do just that because Chad's family is rich anyway. Jacob wants to be a damn rock star. I wanted him to be a doctor."

"How could you do this to him? You and I both know that he has a heart of gold."

"Look. In this world, love can't buy shit. Money makes the world go around. I will let you in on a little secret. He is in love with you, too, and his mother knows it. She pays me to be over there with him. I'd rather be with Chad. You're into white boys. You see that fine ass hunk I have out there. Isn't he fine?"

The only white boy I am into is J.J., I thought.

"What do you mean she pays you?"

"Jacob's dad left her for a pretty, sophisticated black woman. She saw the same traits in Jacob, and she didn't want him to fall for you. He loves you. You're all he talks about. He blames himself for you going to the slammer. He wanted to come and visit you, but that place was too well hidden. He even checked the mailbox every day, looking for a letter from you. You were supposed to serve five months in there, not three years. It was his mom and that lawyer who got you that much time. She wanted J.J. to be gone off to college by the time you got out, but, when you got out early, she was pissed. Smooches," she said as she walked out the door.

29
I Can't Believe This

When I got home, I walked into my room. I didn't see Jessica's car next door. I was going to take a bath and go next door. I didn't care what the crazy lady said. I went to the attic first to get the envelope out of my YDC uniform. I put the envelope under my bed, and I took a shower. I looked at Mama's picture and said, "Thanks for the sign."

Although her evil twin was downstairs, I knew she wasn't Mama. I went downstairs, and she was nowhere to be found. I knocked on J.J.'s door as hard as I could. I was going to let Ms. Johnson have a piece of my mind. J.J. came to the door.

"Come on in," he said as he opened the door.

"Where is mommy dearest?" I asked as I looked around.

"She's shopping," he said as he stretched and yawned.

"J.J., did you know that your mother is the reason for me getting a lengthy sentence?"

"No. What do you mean?"

"She and that sleaze ball lawyer Mr. Martin rigged my time. J.J., I have to talk to you. I am in love with you, and I have to let you know that Jessica's baby isn't yours. I saw Jessica and the real baby's daddy at my job today."

"What?" He said in disbelief.

"She's right," I heard Ms. Johnson say. "That isn't your daughter. I know you're in love with Tasha. I paid Jessica to say that the baby was yours. I didn't want you to leave me like your father did. Does that make me a bad mother, son?"

"Yes," he said as he turned to me. "How could you do this to Tasha Jean, after all this poor girl have been through? Mother, you're going to rot in hell for this one!"

"Son, I'm so sorry. I didn't know what else to do."

"Mother, she lost her mom, and you tried to put her away forever. I'll never forgive you for this!"

"Tasha Jean, I am sorry. Sometimes, a mother has to do what she thinks is right."

"I'm going to live with Dad," J.J said as he ran to his room to fetch some things.

"Tasha Jean, I am so sorry. I really am."

"You have no idea what I went through in there. I was raped. I had to call a racist man master. I had to fight to save my life, and it's all because of you, but you know what? I forgive you, and I love your son to death. We have been best friends since elementary school. I would never do anything to hurt him. I love him too much."

"Here! Take my blackberry, and I will call you from Dad's house," J.J. said as he left. I walked out behind him, and he was sitting in the car, beating on the steering wheel. I got in on the passenger's side.

"Tasha Jean, I've loved you, too, ever since the fifth grade," he said as tears rolled down his face. "I wish I could take back that day when I let Jessica in. I've blamed myself everyday for you going to jail. Because, if I wouldn't have opened the door for her, you wouldn't have gotten in the car with Spyder."

"Don't blame yourself," I said as I caught his tears. "What matters is that we have each other now. I know where a lot of money is. Once I get it, we can move away from this place."

"Tasha Jean, you stay away from that drug money!"

"That's just it. It's unmarked drug money."

"Well, just be careful," he said as he hugged me. "I love you."

He looked me in my eyes.

"I love you, too. I love you now, and I will love you forever."

When he pulled off, I saw a car coming down the road. It was the amber green eyed devil.

30
The Plan

"I have all my team players in action," he said as he got out of the car. One of his team players must have been the crazy lady because she wasn't here.

"I have my tool belt handy," I said sarcastically.

"You will meet me at Spyder's place tomorrow night at eight P.M. sharp."

"Can't wait," I said as I walked into the house. I went in my room, and I opened the envelope and found pictures of me at all different ages. Then, a letter fell out. I opened it up and it read:

Allen Knox,

You know that Tasha Jean is your child.
She looks exactly like you. She even has your smile.
When I gave birth to her, the first thing that I noticed were her eyes,
And you were a lying son of a bitch who didn't take care of our child.
I've been sending you letters almost every day of the year.
I was a virgin when we slept together. I thought that I had made myself clear.
Tasha Jean is a part of you, whether you like it or not.
Y'all even have the same birth mark spot.
When she was born, she was such a bundle of joy.
She had a twin, too, but he didn't make it. It was a boy.
Allen Knox, that little girl didn't ask to be here,
But we'll see what your wife thinks when a little birdie whispers in her ear.

I was shook. Mr. Knox was my daddy! How could he have abused me like that? He knew that I was his daughter, and he still fucked me. Mama told him that I was his daughter. Now, it was all coming back to me. I remembered that he had told me that he killed a nigger bitch, and that nigger bitch was Mama! He said that she had a surprise for him, and he said, when he got there, he had a surprise for her. Mama threatened to go to his wife about me, and he killed her. Mama is dead because of me! All of a sudden, Mama's picture fell off of my nightstand and broke. As I picked it up, I noticed a piece of paper in it. I opened it up and it read:

Tasha Jean,

I know that you thought that I didn't love you, baby,
But the things I went through made me crazy.
I know I caused you a lot of stress,
And I want you to please forgive me for being a pest.
I want you to know that I am so sorry. Please forgive me.
I have my reasons. Plus, only God can judge me.
I should have told you the truth a long time ago, but
There were some terrible things that I didn't want you to know,
Like the fact that your father is a real racist prick,
And he made me his black nigger slave bitch.
If you're reading this letter that means that I'm dead and no longer here.
On the night I told him about you, he said that he'd come back and make himself clear.
People from all different places will come in your face.
My evil twin Annette knows about the millions at Spyder's place.

I felt like Mama was still alive. She loved me but didn't know how to tell me who my daddy was. I couldn't help that I looked just like him, but I had a plan of my own for when I met him there later that night. Even after all the things I had told her, Mrs. Reynolds still hadn't locked him up yet, so it looked like I had to take matters into my own hands. I put on all black and grabbed the tools and headed out the door. I walked through the dark trail in the back. I saw Annette looking around, talking on the phone.

"Where are you going? This place is giving me the creeps," she said to the person on the phone. "You can't turn on the side lanes and go through the wreck?"

Then, she turned around and asked into the dark, "Who is there?"

I threw a screwdriver at her. She ran at me, but I clipped her. She fell to the ground, and I tied her hands behind her back.

"Going somewhere, Grandma? I meant crazy ass Annette! I know who you are."

"How do you know?"

"My mother told me."

"But your mother is dead."

"You're right, but she's with me in spirit. So, what's the plan?" I asked as I pulled out some duct tape. "You know Mr. Knox don't like black people, right? Did you know that he's just using you? Did you know that he's my father?"

"Yes, I know all of that, but guess what, Tasha Jean. I am your mother."

"Don't say that! My mother died! You're the evil twin!"

"Sweetie, listen to me. How do you think the letter got in the picture in your room? This was my plan. I planned this whole thing, and I accidentally got my twin sister killed.

It was the same night that I told AK about you. I knew that he would think that I was her. He never knew about my twin. No one did! I thought of this plan because I wanted to get his ass back. I told Mrs. Reynolds about you and him. She knew who he was, and she tapped all of his phone calls. I had to act different once you got out of jail."

"Well, aren't you sad about your twin being dead?"

"Of course, I am. She was just doing me a favor, and that was to go along with my plan to catch Mr. Knox red handed."

"But how do I know you're my mother?"

"Here! Quick! Grab this phone, and look at the last number that I dialed. It's Mrs. Reynolds number."

Then, I remembered that I had my appointment card on me. I looked at the numbers, and they matched. She was telling the truth!

"Mama, I love you, but there is something that I have to do. I have to kill him. You can watch him beg for his life now because I am going to kill him slowly."

I put duct tape over her mouth because I still couldn't trust her. I didn't know what to believe. I went to the safe, and I opened it. The cash was all there. I quickly closed it back because I heard someone coming.

"I'm here, nigger bitch! Did you pick the safe yet? I'm ready for my cash."

 I tackled him and hit him in the head with the hammer. I got on top of him and said, *"Shut the fuck up and take this death like a man.*
You killed my mother with your own two hands.
No wonder she said that I had devil eyes
Because you were my daddy to my surprise.
Daddy, why didn't you look into my eyes and see

You knew that I was your daughter and you still did all those bad
things to me?
You knew that I was your child,
And you continued to fuck me wild."
Then, he interrupted me and said,
"I was going to kill you after I got the cash.
You were the only one who could get to the stash"
"Fuck the money. You're my daddy. Don't you see?
This isn't how a father and daughter should be.
You thought you killed my mother by slicing her throat,
But it is your own blood that you will choke."
"Baby, please give me the hammer," I heard a familiar voice say.
It was mama and Mrs. Reynolds coming my way.
"Wait a minute! I'm your fucking dad.
The Bible says honor thy mother and father."
"That's just it. You're not a father.
You fucked me and made me your slave.
You better start praying to God that your soul He'll save
Because God witnessed all of the shit that you put me through,
And he's the one who helped me get revenge on you.
You better say a prayer, and you better say it quick.
Oops! Times up! Your neck I'm about to split."

    "Tasha Jean, it's over. Let the law deal with him now. You don't want it to end it like this."
    "Yes, I do! Mrs. Reynolds, is that lady really my mama?"
    "Scouts honor," she said as she put her hand over her heart.
    Mama walked over and looked at him. When he saw her face, he almost had a heart attack.
    "Nigger bitch, I killed you with my bare hands!"

"It's all over Special Agent Utah," Ms. Reynolds said as she pulled out some cuffs from behind her back.

"You knew about this all along?" I asked with the hammer still at his neck.

"Yes, I'm afraid so, but your mother came up with the brilliant idea. She lost her twin sister, but he's going to die in jail."

I got off of him and ran into Mama's arms.

"And just to think I respected you," she said as she cuffed him.

"Wait a minute! How does he get to have two names?" I asked.

"One of his names, he uses undercover when he befriends the dope boys. He was a dirty cop, and I have been after him for years."

"We're safe now, baby," Mama said as she hugged me.

31
Guilty! Guilty! Guilty!

Mrs. Reynolds hauled him off to jail. I asked Mama why she didn't she let me see J.J. She said because she didn't want me to run off with him. She had used me for bait. Her plan really worked. I had my Mama back! When we got back home, J.J. and his dad was there along with Mrs. Reynolds. We all sat in the living room. Mrs. Reynolds explained that I would be going to court soon. I had to testify against all three of the perpetrators from YDC. She told me that the warden wasn't supposed to be running that YDC facility like that.

I'd never seen J.J.'s dad before.

"Tasha Jean, this is my dad Jacob Sr., and this is Tanya, the sophisticated woman that he married," he said as he pointed at Mrs. Reynolds.

"What about the thirty million?"

"What thirty million?" they all said.

"I know where thirty million dollars is."

"Are you serious?" they all asked me at once.

"Follow me," I said as I headed out the screen door.

We all walked to Spyder's house, and I opened the safe.

"You deserve it," J.J's dad said.

They helped me and Mama carry the money to our house. It took us five hours to count all of that money with the help of the money counting machine. J.J. was right by my side.

Court came around sooner than I expected. All of the girls were in the courtroom to testify. Sticky was there, looking like a girl. She didn't look like a boy-girl anymore. Jennifer didn't come. She was in the studio recording a CD for a major record label. Kenya was there. The court compensated all the families of the girls' who had killed themselves. The warden and Mr. Knox and Ms. Allgood were dressed in orange jumpsuits with shackles on their feet. They wore uniforms with numbers on them now. It was now time for them to be sentenced.

"Do any of you girls have anything to say?" the judge asked.

The only one went up was Sticky. She said, "First, I want to apologize to Tasha Jean for picking fights with her at the YDC. Secondly, I want to ask God to have mercy on my mother's soul."

She looked at Ms. Allgood. I knew that she was her daughter because she favored her more than any other girl in there. Plus, they looked so much alike.

"Mother, I am glad that I found God in that place. I know you can't help who you are, but you made me think that your way of living was right, and it was wrong. Tasha Jean, you have saved so many girls. If it wasn't for you being so courageous, none of us would be here today."

"That's right," the judge said. "Do any more girls want to speak?"

No one stood up.

"Do any of you three want to speak?" she asked as she turned to three convicts.

Mr. Knox stood up and said, "Y'all still a bunch of nigger bitches!"

"Order in the court," the judge said as she hit the gavel. "Order in the court! I hereby sentence you all to life in prison without the possibility of parole."

The courtroom was overwhelmed! Everyone was clapping and jumping up and down. Sticky Fingers came over to hug me. She wasn't a bad person after all. She was just doing what she thought was best because her mother had showed her that. My mama told me that, ever since she had notified Mr. Knox about him being my father, she kept trying to come up with a plan that would take him down. She said that she'd been plotting on this master plan for years. She told me that, one day, her twin showed up, and she decided to let her in on the plan.

She even told me that, on the night that I thought that it was her putting me out, it was really Annette. She said that they would take turns sitting on the sofa, and I didn't know the difference because they were identical. She said that she didn't know that Mr. Knox would go as far as killing someone. I was so glad that she was alive. She did what she did to bring the bad guys down, and I was glad that God had helped me not to break. Mr. Knox was charged with Spyder's death because the autopsy showed that he was alive at the scene of the accident. Mr. Knox was the first one there, and he had cut his head off. He was the one who took the three other kilos of cocaine. He was also charged with my Aunt Annette's murder. He was responsible for all of the girls who had killed themselves in the YDC. He got the death penalty.

Mrs. Reynolds asked me if I want to sit in and watch his execution. I said no. I had too many memories of him in my head already. Mama, on the other hand, said that, when the time came, she would be there with bells on. She owed it to Annette. Mama told me that, when she was a teenager, her mother had put her out. She said that she ran to a bar, and that was where she was allured by Mr. Knox. She said that he'd told her that he would put her up in a hotel to sleep for the night. She said that he raped her and made her his sex slave. She told me that she got away and swore on her life that she would find him and bring him down one day.

She said that that was her first time having sex, and she got pregnant with me. She apologized for putting me through all of the things that she had put me through. I forgave her. I understood that she did what she did to try and protect me. I must admit that she had the perfect plan. I was trying to think of a plan myself to bring him down, but mothers always know best.

As time went on, I wanted to do something that could help girls who'd gotten in trouble. J.J. and I had more than enough money. I decided to round up a few of the girls who had been in the YDC with me. I told them that I had jobs for them. I wanted Sticky Fingers to be in charge. She had really changed; she'd even got a man! The name of my facility was called LISTEN TO OUR LITTLE LADIES YOUTH DETENTION CENTER.

We could save plenty of lives. Who could be better counselors than us? We'd all been to hell and back. We could prevent young girls from making the same mistakes that we had.

Even though I was violated in that crazy youth detention center, it didn't kill me. It had made me stronger, and I was one tough cookie. I was so glad that God used me in this way.

J.J. and I got married, and we bought us a Victorian home. He patched things up with his mom, and she accepted me after all. He told her that, if she didn't accept me, he would be out of her life for good. Jacob Sr. and Mrs. Reynolds didn't live too far from us. They were excellent grandparents.

Mama moved in with us to help us take care of our kids. I was pregnant for the third time. Jacob the third was eight years old, and the twins Justin and Zack were five. And I was about to give birth to our fourth son Jeremy. God showed me that dreams really do come true.

About The Author

Antoinette Tunique Smith was born in San Francisco, California and raised in ATL, where she still resides. She is blessed with five children who are known as the five lights of her life: Pinky, Driah, Clyde, Chicken and Fat Boy.

She would like people to know that it doesn't matter where you come from, you can be whatever you wanna be. Just believe in God. There is a God!

Thanks &
Much respect,
Antoinette Smith

OTHER TITLES BY ANTOINETTE SMITH
*DADDY'S FAVORITE POP
*MARRIED: SNEAKY BLACK WOMAN

UPCOMING BOOKS BY ANTOINETTE SMITH
*I'M A DRAG NOT A FAG
*BLACK-OUT ON BANKHEAD
*I'M BI Y LIE
*WOMEN R DOGS TOO?
*I WISH I WAS RAISED
*MY LIFE, MY PAIN (BOOK OF POEMS)

www.straighttothepointbooks.com

acansing2000@yahoo.com